Praise for William Dickerson's novel *No Alternative*:

"A sympathetic coming-of-age story deeply embedded in '90s music. Reflective, unafraid of big-picture pronouncements—'nothing is more do-it-yourself than suicide.' The cool, casual tone results in knockout diagnoses of the '90s teenage condition: 'You feel older as a teenager than you will ever feel in your entire life.'"

—*Kirkus Reviews*

"The novel—with its clear-eyed glimpse into the lives of a troubled family—satisfies."

—*Publishers Weekly*

"Simultaneously brutal and funny, caustic and caring, *No Alternative* is a sacrament to be shared by all the survivors who grew up at the tail end of the fragmenting century."

—Jack O'Connell, author of *"The Resurrectionist"*

"Pungent insights and quotable dialogue abound in this novel, which, in the end, movingly dramatizes the ability of art to transcend death and other human tragedies."

—*Indie Reader*

"If his future material is as full of idiosyncratic life as *No Alternative*, then Dickerson will undoubtedly be a writer to follow."

—*Independent Publisher*

THE DREAMACHINE
LA MACHINE DE RÊVE
ドリーム・マシーン

WILLIAM DICKERSON

Editors: Rachel Hoffman, Dwight Moody and William Wolfe
Cover Design: Matthew Revert

Kettle of Letters Press
Los Angeles, CA

ISBN: 9780985188658

10 9 8 7 6 5 4 3 2 1

ACKNOWLEDGMENTS

Writing this book could not have been possible without the support of my family and friends, specifically my wife, Rachel, and my longtime collaborator, Dwight Moody.

This novel owes a debt of gratitude to the Beat Generation, to Paris, France—*the City of Light*—and to the boundless enigma that is the human brain. It also owes a debt to Brion Gysin, the creator of the Dreamachine device, through which inspired me to dream this dream into words on paper.

I want to thank my parents for always encouraging me to keep writing.

Always keep writing.

DEDICATION

This novel is dedicated to my wife and child.

INTRODUCTION

THE DREAMACHINE embedded itself in my consciousness in early 2005 via *The New York Times, Home & Garden* section, in an article entitled "Décor by Timothy Leary," written by Mark Allen. In the article, Allen wrote of the cylindrical device:

> Besides the trippy visual effects, the device is said to induce an 'alpha state'—a state conducive to lucid dreaming or intense daydreaming—in people who face the cylinder with their eyes closed as it spins around a bright light.

My interest was instantly piqued. Like many people, I'm fascinated by dreams. What are they? What causes them? Why do we dream? How do they affect us both psychologically and physiologically? On a philosophical level, there is a distinction between our dreams and our reality, but how vast is that distinction, or how narrow? Can our dreams influence our reality? Maybe more interestingly, can we train ourselves in waking life so that our dream life is more compelling, and more real, a practice referred to as lucid dreaming. I've attempted lucid dreaming in the past, but with only very limited success. It was an effort that seemed to require a lot of time for results that were unpredictable and difficult to measure. The idea that a device comprised of a cylindrical tube with holes cut into it that spun around a light source (equivalent to wrapping cardboard around the platter of an old record player and suspending a naked light bulb into it) could grant access to the subconscious, while in a conscious state, seemed far-fetched. But because I'm interested in dreams, and how they might influence my creative work, it was an idea I couldn't set aside.

Allen shined a spotlight in print on the person who was in the business of making and selling Dreamachines. That person was David Woodard:

> Mr. Woodard was able to borrow the original Dream-achine templates and built his first one in 1989; within a few years word of mouth and modest advertising led to a full-fledged business. He made two for William Burroughs and has made others for celebrities including Iggy Pop, Beck and Kurt Cobain. Mr. Woodard charges $500 for a basic model with a cylinder of acid-free matting board. (The cylinder surrounds a 150-watt bulb, which is mounted in the center of a wood base holding a motor that spins the cylinder at 80 rpm) Custom models, with cylinders made from steel, copper or cocobolo wood—or even covered in ermine fur—can cost as much as $3000.

The product and its accompanying mystique sounded a bit hippy-dippy and I thought I caught the whiff of patchouli in the air, an herb with origins in the mint family. Had the newspaper been soaked in this patchouli substance? In his novel, *In Search of Lost Time,* the French writer Marcel

Proust suggested that smell was the primary sense that triggered the recollection of distant memories. I had no memory of patchouli. This was not an instance of the Proustian Phenomenon.

Perhaps I had smelled the odor in a dream and forgotten—the subconscious is a vault that consciousness cannot open. But with the Dreamachine, it seemed I might be able to do just that.

Furthermore, while patchouli was an idea I associated with a certain era of time, a particular counterculture, my culture was part of the equation as well. There were rumblings that Nirvana frontman Kurt Cobain—an admirer of William Burroughs, the famous beat writer, who ritualistically used the Dreamachine and wrote quite extensively about it in his books—not only owned the device, but had used it up to 72 hours straight, in his greenhouse, in the days leading up to his suicide. Some even went so far as to suggest that it was the machine that made him do it.

In an article published in *High Times* in April of 1996, writers Tim Kenneally and Steve Bloom described receiving a fax in December of 1994 from a Seattle-based group called *Friends Understanding Kurt* that made mention of the device. They claimed that the device, which Kurt had procured only months before he killed himself, was "the catalyst in his unbelievably tragic, untimely death." The article went on to say, "To this day Courtney ponders whether the Dreamachine is really responsible for Kurt's death…If Kurt had not come into contact with its manufacturer, he would be with us today."

Who did Kurt Cobain procure this device from?

David Woodard.

Woodard was quoted in the same article as saying with respect to Cobain: "the Dreamachine helped him to see that he was beginning to fall apart as a cultural figure…I pictured the suicide as being informed by an inner voice which was made audible through his experiences with the Dreamachine," he explained. "Yes, the Dreamachine played a part." While this kind of information, real or not, might have deterred potential consumers, it made me even more curious.

I decided to contact Woodard through his website and inquire into his Dreamachine products. In an email exchange, he explained a little about the creation of his version of the machine:

> The material I use for the cylinder is an acid-free, 2-ply museum matting board. It is resilient, but I would say rather fragile. So long as you keep your machine away from unruly large animals, high-functioning autistic persons, etc., you should be fine. Yes, the base is wood—usually pine, sometimes mohagany [sic] or oak, depending on season / availability / whim.

As our correspondence continued, he went on further to explain the effects of using the machine:

> Although techniques and effects are, to a degree, specific to the user, the machine's rudimentary effects are universal—e.g., the effect of what appears to be an animated Persian rug eventually segueing into quasi-cinematic images. I am providing a basic set of instructions with your machine. However, I am also in the process of collecting subjective reports and suggestions—for publication. In a reversal of your question, perhaps you would, when time permits, send a report on your experience for inclusion.

I ended up ordering a Museum model, a spinning copper cylinder affixed to a Sirari Rosewood base. Woodard generously gave me half off the $3000 list price—rent is high in Los Angeles, and I was in graduate school. I promptly paid him the $1500, and almost as promptly, never heard from the man again.

Three months passed. I emailed him once a week. No response of any kind. I wasn't that worried at first; I guess I'd given him leeway because he was an artist and I had commissioned him to work on a custom project, though he did say it would only take three weeks. He was a known artist with what I thought was a decent reputation—*The New York Times* had validated him.

I started to reconsider that notion.

The way I ordered the item was atypical. Not unusual to me, since the Dreamachine wasn't a typical product. I paid Woodard directly via my credit card to initiate the commission. This was before PayPal was a transactional ubiquity. In other words, there was no safety net. There was just the trust between one artist and another.

The moment that trust dissipated, I did what any self-respecting artist would do with no other option left: investigate.

The only phone number I was able to dig up in the various emails we exchanged leading up to the order turned out to be long distance. Long distance as in not in this country. The country code belonged to Paraguay.

Paraguay. I had little to no knowledge of Paraguay, other than the fact that it was somewhere in South America and they were known for producing quite a soccer team over the years. I called the number I had found and a Paraguayan woman answered the phone. She spoke English, thankfully, but bristled at the mention of David Woodard's name:

"I do not know where Mr. David is…[a long and rather

uncomfortable pause] he owes me a lot of money."

Apparently, he had lodged at this woman's residence for an unspecified amount of time, until she demanded payment for said lodgings. Then he disappeared into the night. David Woodard had absconded with my cash and fled to Paraguay. While on the surface, it almost seemed like a whimsical Mosquito Coast adventure that I unwillingly funded, it turned out that this kookery was much more endemic.

Woodard's modus operandi for travelling to Paraguay appeared to be the desire to start, or more accurately, to restart, an Aryan colony.

In the late Nineteenth Century, Bernard Forster and Elisabeth Nietzsche, sister of Frederick, and a handful of other Germans settled into the remote jungles of Paraguay and called their collective experiment "Nueva Germania." The experiment's goal was the creation of a racially pure utopia that intended to give rise to the "rebirth of the human race." They hoped that their mission of reestablishing a pure bloodline would spread throughout, and eventually usurp, the entire South American continent. However, as with so many utopian outposts, the starkness of the environment proved too difficult for an extended residence and stymied their attempt to achieve their vision.

Some families were able to survive in the jungle, but many died of disease and others moved back to Germany—Elisabeth Nietzsche included. The settlement continued to exist, but it certainly did not thrive. There was a slight resurgence in popularity circa the end of World War II, when Nazi war criminals were on the run and looking for a new place to call their home. Perhaps, it was to be Paraguay. Josef Mengele, the infamous Nazi physician who experimented on concentration camp inmates at Auschwitz, fled to Paraguay after the war.

Elisabeth Nietzsche committed suicide before she was able to see Paraguay shelter Nazis, but she counseled and supported the Nazi Party until her death in 1935. Hitler granted her a state memorial service.

At the time of my Dreamachine purchase, David Woodard ostensibly took up the time-honored cause of attempting to restore racial purity to the Germanic race. In his words, posted on SFGate.com: "Nueva Germania represents an aesthetic sanctuary conceived by Wagner; a place where Aryans could peaceably go to experience life and pursue the advancement of Germanic culture." Woodard planned to build a "Dreamachine factory" on the site where Josef Mengele, who was responsible for the deaths of hundreds of thousands of Jews and other Nazi victims, once lived.

He was indeed funding his cause, but he was doing it through fraudulent orders of Dreamachines, not the fulfillment of them.

There was something apropos about this idea. I had been robbed in two different ways: robbed of my money and robbed of the ideal that the Dreamachine represented. It was clear that this particular craftsman meant to use the monies he had stolen from me, and potentially others, to advance an ideal that represented the perfect nightmare for so many people, namely the Jewish people, for so many years.

The idea of a Dreamachine, the device originally created by Brion Gysin and Ian Sommerville, that was brought into the light of day by William S. Burroughs—before it was ever connected to Woodard—still very much fascinated me. This experience reminded me that the flipside of the dream is, in fact, the nightmare; that while the idea of dialing up a dream on demand was alluring, the dialer also assumed the risk of not getting the dream, but getting the nightmare. The dream and the nightmare are two sides of the same subconscious coin.

Some years later, I was finally able to buy a Dreamachine from the first company to be officially sanctioned by Brion Gysin's estate. I began experimenting with the light it emitted and recorded its effects on both conscious and subconscious time as I experienced it. The goal is the same: to achieve the dream, to realize the dream, to understand the dream, while weighing the risk of triggering the nightmare that's lurking inside, implanted from birth, from a virus, from culture and society at large, waiting for its chance to be let out like some kind of rogue genie in a bottle.

There was a more recent article on Nueva Germania in *The New York Times*—nearly ten years after it published its piece on the Dreamachine—that outlined the experiment's failed mission and shined a light on those families still living in the region, who are still attempting, with abject futility, to advance the cause of purification. David Woodard was not mentioned in the article. Nor were any Dreamachine factories.

I have found, both personally and professionally, that reality can be so stark and unfathomable in its relentlessness that many people proactively seek an escape from it. That's the dream. The nightmare, however, seems to be: what if the escape from reality is the reality itself?

CHAPTER ONE

T HE STALACTITE heels of stilettos clacked along a cobblestone street. From the look of it alone, this street existed somewhere in Europe, perhaps London, or France, or Prague. Or it could very well be New York, someplace in the Meatpacking District, near that bar where Dylan Thomas drank himself to death. Couldn't say for sure, but it just had that feel. The surroundings possessed that old world, gothic romanticism, where the glow of the sun—or the street lamps—wraps itself around the curves of the stones in the pavement. On this day, however, the reflection of the sun on the stones was subdued. It rang of the unnatural, like the life of the streets was being repressed. The tapered wooden heels of these shoes were the only things that demonstrated a discernable color, the color of bright red, quite near florescent.

The pair of stilettos passed through the double doors of a hotel, an old building situated in the middle of a block of identical looking beige buildings, just steps from a building on the corner that could be the Flatiron building's shorter and stouter sibling. Though there was no channel of water in peripheral sight, there was an unmistakable breeze wafting through the adjacent alleyways that moistened the skin and swathed the surface of the streets with a sheen that reflected the diffused sun in a way that suggested there was.

The stilettos proceeded their march up a claustrophobic set of stairs, the spiral kind—each wooden step boasted the imprint of the shoe bottoms of previous generations and generations previous to theirs, imprints that served as proof of the existence of those who came before. When the pair of shoes reached the top floor, they advanced with metronomic stride down a narrow hallway and past a multitude of doors. Upon first glance, the doors all appeared to be identical. As the shoes came to a momentary rest, they pivoted toward a door at the tail end of the stretch of corridor.

The tunnel vision, the vignette, the stereoscopic viewer, through which the backs of these stilettos were framed, floated upwards, gliding up the length of her legs and rising above her back, until it seized its view behind the sinewy red hair of this nameless woman's head.

This woman—this *mystery* woman—opened the door, walked inside the room, and shut it securely behind her, almost as swiftly as she opened it. It was like she'd done this a million times before, the action, reflexive; but something, some *thing* was very different this time. The only thing remaining in the wake of these imagistic fragments was the brass-plated number on the outside of the door: 604. It was as though the numbers had been plunged into a fire and their glowing outline had been held outstretched to brand whosoever provoked the smoldering numbers with a glance of one's eyes.

Jasper Keepnews startled awake in his bed, springing himself up.

The remnants of the number 604 were baked into the backs of his retinas. Jasper tried blinking them away. But that never worked. Blinking doesn't reverse the blinking, the disappearance and reappearance of the numbers, which were blinking like a short-circuiting clock constructed of Russian nixie tubes. The warm orange glow of the phosphorescent numbers lit the insides of his eyes like a welder working the inner surface of a concave sphere.

"Another bad dream?"

He blinked again—he couldn't quite help himself—this time at the seemingly disembodied voice emanating from the person lying on the mattress beside him. The voice belonged to his wife Paige, his bedfellow, who was in the midst of rousing from her short-lived slumber.

Jasper rubbed his face, sweating profusely, "It's no big deal." His breathing said just the opposite; it was so heavy that with each inhale, he sucked in droplets of the sweat that had funneled into the deltas at the corners of his mouth.

Paige dropped a gentle hand on his chest, her palm a little pillow of comfort and ease. She was petite, Asian American, a bookseller by trade, and by attire. She sported cat-eye glasses when she was not in bed, though had come to use them liberally as a means to lure others with predilections for librarians and a fondness for the Dewey Decimal System into bed. Jasper certainly was a sucker for it, for that there was no doubt—whenever she wasn't wearing them, he tried to imagine she was. He tried doing this now, but without much success.

"You need to blow off more steam," Paige said.

"I'll be fine."

Jasper shook it off. Both his body and his mind were in his bed—that much was clear as a church bell. He was not in a hotel room, nor was he in a city that was foreign to him. He was sitting upright, in his bed, at home.

He turned his head, rolled his shoulders back, the fluid between his joints audibly popping, and smiled at his wife. She smiled sleepily back at him.

***

Jasper hunched over the granite kitchen counter, noticeably fatigued, shaking processed flakes of Folgers Instant coffee into a ceramic mug shaped like a Rubik's Cube. It was unsolved, a mosaic of unique blue, green, yellow, orange, red and white patterns of squares on each side. He was a middle-aged man who looked to be in damn good shape, despite his sluggishness. He didn't often hunch. This morning was particularly bad; the dreams were getting to him. They always got to him, but now they were *getting* to him. He regarded himself a reserved man—he took pride in that regard when he was aware of such a thing—and it showed in his physicality: he wore his body like a suit he was trying hard not to wrinkle. It offset the limp.

He had a tendency to stare at things. When he made his coffee in the morning, he'd often stare at the counter, into the chasm of the pinkish-grey granite, the nooks and spaces in the amalgamated sediment. It reminded him of lava rock, and lacking the knowledge of how granite becomes the granite that's compressed into kitchen counters, he often wondered if there might be some volcanic element in the mix somewhere, like the accidental almond in the jar of peanut butter.

But this morning, he didn't stare at the counter. He stared at the small flat-screen television situated in the corner where the counter met the electric stove; the appliance was staring back at him with a commercial for the prescription antidepressant *Tymatrope*. It was unclear whether staring at the TV—as opposed to the counter—would wake him up or lull him back into his earlier sleep. Either way, it didn't much matter; he kept on staring at it—

A jubilant father hoisted his young daughter onto his shoulders in the center of a lush field, grass as green as emeralds, steering her toward the trunk of an enormous apple tree. The tree was resplendent, its bark alive; it looked like a piece of plant life from a Norman Rockwell painting. As the man nodded his head encouragingly toward the hanging fruit, the youngster balanced herself on her tippy-toes, reached up and plucked an apple from a nearby branch, taking a big old bite of it without a moment's hesitation. As she sunk her porcelain teeth into the apple's gleaming red skin, her father smiled and the narrator intoned:

"Trusted By Doctors, Making Your Life Better—*Tymatrope*: Swing from the Tree Of Life."

The girl joined the actor playing her father in his ham-fisted bit of exaggerated smiling, this time performing it straight to camera, *breaking the fourth wall*, as they say in the theatre.

Jasper stared at the little ingénue on screen; unlike his previous stare, this was a stare that might be described as possessing a touch of longing. Might be, because even Jasper wasn't sure, or if it was that type of look, he was unsure when the look started and when it would stop. There was no doubt this feeling, or whatever it was that he felt, was directed toward the child, who seemed about the age of five—more likely she was an eight year-old, playing the role of a five year-old. Without a doubt, the advertisers intended for such an emotional result. He blinked his eyes rapidly before changing the channel and bringing this feeling to an end. The programming on the tube—well, it wasn't a tube anymore, right, more like *the LCD*, or *the plasma*; in the kitchen, it's probably *the LCD*—switched to an ongoing press conference, one that was being broadcast from the national stage of the theatre of politics.

President of the United States, Surina Rafferty—the first biracial Hispanic female leader of the free world—addressed the swarm of media wielding their microphones and cameras in the White House Press Room. The press had always been particularly hard on her, at least from Jasper's perspective. It didn't help that she preferred to talk to them herself, often tagging out her press secretary and interacting with reporters, as she decided to do this morning.

"The plan that I am proposing is estimated to cut the deficit in half by the end of the decade." Rafferty exclaimed.

There was a cacophony of inquisitive shouts—decorum in the White House, particularly among the press, has been in steady decline for years. However, one question bled through the rest: "You're confident that cutting the defense budget is the answer? Are you at all afraid this'll weaken the military?" A young male reporter asked.

"The problem isn't the military. The problem is the contractors—big businesses making a killing off the killing of our nation's young men and women overseas."

The kettle hissed ever so slightly, but it was just enough for a lukewarm cup of joe. It was also just enough to drown out the predictable vociferousness from the reporters calling for some elaboration. Jasper reached for the kettle, poured a flume of warmish water into his cup as he continued to lean a forearm on the counter.

"It costs 100 million dollars to build one SX-51 Blackwing Bomber," Rafferty continued. "Exorbitant military spending is a thing of the past, a result of fear-mongering and private sector war profiteering. I want to take that one hundred million out of the pockets of Applied Precision

Electronics and put it back into the pockets of the tax-payers who are out of work."

Jasper stirred his coffee, plunked the plastic top back on the instant coffee tin, and pushed it into a corner next to a fancy, and not to mention sparkling clean, Cuisinart coffee-maker. He scrutinized this mechanical wonder of convenience, but still couldn't help but think his instant coffee was far more convenient. It's also convenient to keep the tin next to the machine, even though he doesn't use the machine, much to the chagrin of his wife whose occasional and, all things considered, minor fits of anxiety solely involve objects—appliances, foodstuffs, anything of practical utility—being out of place in the kitchen.

"Why'd we bother getting that fancy thing with the grinder if I still use this instant shit?"

"I don't know why you're asking me that question," Paige said, from around the corner. She shuffled into the kitchen with a rather grubby stack of used books under her arm. She plunked the hardcovers down on the kitchen's center island, which boasted a matching granite top, and took a seat in a chair.

Jasper turned to her, sipping his coffee, "Tastes like dirt."

"And you keep drinking it."

Paige smirked as Jasper picked up the book on the top of the pile and glanced at the upside-down dust jacket: *On The Road* by Jack Kerouac.

"Any of the dirt left?" Paige asked, as she grabbed the book out of his hand, inserting it back into the stack.

"On the counter."

Without any consideration to its urgency or potential ramifications to the nation, or the world, she proceeded to change the channel on the TV from the White House briefing to a benign, and unquestionably catchy, Folgers commercial on another network. Jasper chuckled as he looked toward the screen; he couldn't help himself, besides, laughter naturally releases endorphins—it made him feel good, kind of like the caffeine in his coffee.

"That's why," Paige said.

"Touché."

Paige shook her head at the television, and then she poured some coffee for herself. Jasper's laughter died down, but its ricochet lingered.

***

It was a near picture-perfect day in Seattle, Washington; the sun was shining, which is a rarity in these parts. It was, in other words, a perfect day for a round of disc golf.

That's exactly what the marketers of the game's discs want you to believe. It's not often that Seattle's climate is clear enough to allow for a proper game of disc golf, so one must seize the moment while one can. When a day like this presents itself to its residents, options of outdoor activity are plentiful, and the choice of option is an important choice because it might be a while before another day of choices like this comes along again. It is this choice that advertising executives toil over in boardrooms, in ergonomic chairs behind their sleek minimalist desks, and out there in the trenches testing the products they're consigned to push.

While Jasper was not one of these executives, he wasn't toiling any less than they were. He was a humble facilitator hired by these executives to be, for all intents and purposes, a slave to their marketing strategies. Thoughts of strategies similar to the one reliant on weather were passing through his brain, more specifically because his colleague, Cary Bryan, was floating these thoughts through the air and into

Jasper's brain because his account was the disc golf account and he needed someone to play with—and test his client's discs with—today. Cary, a hipster-spun cosmopolitan with slicked back white hair, was about the same age as Jasper, but he looked older for obvious follicular reasons. He used the lack of pigment in his hair to convey an air of wisdom among the clients he was trying to impress, which was not dissimilar to the personal rationale Paige employed with the sporting of her eyeglasses.

The two of them, the two web designers, stood alongside each other on a massive disc golf course. Disc golf wasn't so much a sport or an activity as it was a culture, or a lifestyle choice—don't dare refer to a disc as a *Frisbee* to a disc golfer—and it was this choice that Bryan, and a reluctant Jasper, attempted to pour themselves into, if only for a handful of morning hours.

"Sounds more like a dream, than a nightmare," Cary said, as he heaved a plastic disc across the fertile fairway. It hovered effortlessly over the boundless blades of grass below.

"You would think," Jasper responded, in a somewhat sarcastic tone. The tone was unlike him.

"At least the way you're describing her legs to me."

Jasper smirked, "There's something not right about it. I don't know. I can't describe the feeling, but it felt kind of ominous."

It was Jasper's turn to throw. He gripped a disc, coiled his body, all while Cary scrutinized his approach—really paid attention to his form; it was as if he were studying him.

"Sounds like you need to get laid," Cary said.

"Well," Jasper laughed, "to be honest, we haven't been very active in that department."

"Really?"

"We really haven't. When Paige found out we couldn't have kids, it just became low priority, I guess."

"Do you want children?"

Jasper smiled thinly at Cary then whipped his arm forward, channeling a skeletal spring in his elbow, and launched the disc. The men watched the disc float through the sky as it left Cary's attempt, a commendable attempt, squarely in the dust.

"For what it's worth, I'd give my little ones back if I could," Cary said, his eyes glued to the ascending spinning object that was battling gravity's pull. "I thought you never played this game before?"

"Not bad for a keyboard-jockey, huh?"

"Not bad at all," Cary replied, a wheel or two rotating in his head. "Hey, why don't you take the reigns on this account? I have a pretty full plate right now."

Jasper smiled, a little less thinly than he smiled before, as he reached behind his back and grabbed a cane leaning against a tree stump. He limped up the fairway as energetically as he could.

Having returned to the office, Jasper sat diligently at his computer writing a succession of code. His cubicle was littered with discs, photos of picturesque courses and miscellaneous disc golf paraphernalia. The mountain of promotional schwag consumed the one personal item on his desk: a picture of him and Paige at the Space Needle, at the very top of the slender, alien structure. It would probably be a better allocation of space to display a picture of them against the backdrop of some far-off exotic location, some overt contrast to his present locale and routine—not to discount the aesthetic pleasure of, and amusement derived from, Seattle's most celebrated landmark, but a beach and some palm trees might have been nice. The picture did, in fact, feature Washington's spectacular Mount Rainier in the background. It was just that they hadn't had much time to get away since the wedding. Jasper was inundated with work, which, let's face it, was only a good thing in his ultra-competitive line of work. Paige also labored round-the-clock at her used bookstore, which she co-owned with a junior-year roommate from college—they had spearheaded their undergrad's most popular book club, *Once Upon a Time*, and running a store together had been a joint dream of theirs, humble as that dream might have been in this nation of gargantuan aspirations. Jasper and Paige would take their honeymoon, eventually; when things died down.

Cary rolled his imitation Herman Miller Aeron Chair out of the adjacent cubicle, "It's kind of a dumb game, isn't it?" He reclined back in it, peeking over Jasper's shoulder, "Not to mention, my arm is fucking killing me. Can barely lift the damn thing."

"That's pathetic," Jasper replied, as he blazed through some more code.

"I'm hoping the website I'm building for that pot dispensary in San Francisco will provide some free samples. My muscles sure could use some."

"Check this out." Jasper pressed a few keys, prompting a colorful homepage for Aurora Discs to pop up on screen. Cary leaned in, laying his eyes on the catchphrase.

Aurora Discs… Spinning you into orbit.

The slogan was perched above a disc modeled after the moon, which cruised high above a serene disc golf course. The design was a take on George Méliès's film *A Trip To The Moon*, the first sci-fi film in history. The famous image from the film, a spaceship in the shape of a bullet landing in the eye of the moon, had been rebooted into an image of a silver disc puncturing the pockmarked celestial body. Jasper hadn't been aware of this film before he typed "famous images of the moon" into his search engine, but he was instantly intrigued by the imagery and the onion-layered history of the film itself, which apparently was one of the first *pataphysical* films—pataphysical defined as the science of imaginary solutions. He had jotted down in a notebook the phrase: *a practice that sought to expose the illogicality of logical thinking.* In the case of Méliès's *A Trip To The Moon*, it seemed to mock the scientists, and their underlying science of space by depicting the moon as the face of a human being, a mortal man.

Jasper realized he was probably overthinking things a bit and spent a lot of time making notes; he had a desk drawer filled with them. Recently, he had started gravitating toward those small black notebooks—the kind with the rounded corners, sewn pages and silk bookmarks. The ones Paige had begun selling at her store were small enough to pocket, and he liked the idea of their diminutiveness about as much as he liked writing in them. The truth was he got paid to think just so much: "I'm not in charge of the marketing, I just push the buttons and try to make the sites look pretty. Or as pretty as I can."

Cary turned back to his computer, snickering under his breath, the air in his nose chortling out. The project was on the cheesy side, but he could tell Jasper was enjoying it to the best of his ability. In fact, it was more intellectually challenging than the bulk of the work they're typically contracted to do, in that it referenced something foreign and fairly obscure, and he should be happy about that. If an employee couldn't lose himself in his life's work, what was left for him to lose himself in while sitting at the same desk, staring at the same computer, and eating the same chicken parmigiana sandwich for lunch on a daily basis?

"Let me ask you a question: do I look like a hippy to you?" Cary asked.

"Far from it."

"Exactly! Which is why I can't understand why I keep getting these hippie accounts. I got the dope dealers, now I got this Beatnik artist who builds these things—these Dreamachines."

"Dream... Machine?"

"One word, connected at the 'm,' but yes," Cary said. "Have you read much Burroughs?"

"William S. Burroughs? No, I don't think I've read him."

"He wrote a lot about this thing; supposedly it inspired him." Cary pointed at his computer screen, on which displayed a *New York Times* article, the *Arts & Leisure* section. "Inside the cylinder is a light." He scrolled down to a picture of an actual Dreamachine. "As the outside spins, it produces a flicker. Viewers stare into it, but they do it with their eyes closed."

"Staring with closed eyes?"

"See! That's the brilliance of it. The science behind the machine is that it syncs you up to your brain's alpha waves, the frequency of REM sleep, the frequency that tunes you into your dreams. Supposed to give you access to all of your dreams ... while you're awake."

This revelation struck a cord with Jasper, particularly in light of his recent troubles with sleeping. Dreams were becoming more and more synonymous with the troubles.

"I did some research on the inventor of this thing," Cary continued. "He's another Beat writer, like Burroughs. He described his first interaction with the device as 'sweeping him out of time' and predicted it would open a new era of vision, giving people access to, what he referred to as, the 'Human Programme.'" He grinned, and it was a wide one. "Here's the kicker: he said that it allows viewers to see everything that can be seen, or has been seen, or *will* be seen."

"Sounds like he's speaking of the 'collective unconscious.'"

"He's speaking of... the future."

Jasper laughed, maybe a little too much, "Have you been smoking some of that weed from your pot dispensary client?!"

"Yeah, I'm skeptical about the whole clairvoyance thing myself, but imagine if it can unlock whatever it is that's up here..." As Cary knocked a knuckle against his head, he looked over at Jasper, and then pointed his finger at him enthusiastically, "Hey! Maybe you should give it a spin around the block. Might help with those nightmares—who the hell knows."

Jasper sighed, but the electronic bing of Cary's cell phone interrupted his exasperation. Cary slipped the device out of his leather belt holster and glanced at the text responsible for the intruding notification.

"Shit. I gotta pick up the kid," Cary said. "Patti's held up." He looked up at Jasper, pleadingly, "Can you cover for me?"

Jasper squinted. Cary took that as a yes. How else could he take it? He was certainly not going to leave it.

"Thanks, Jasp."

As Cary scurried down the hall, Jasper rolled his chair over to his co-worker's computer. He scanned *The New York Times* article Cary left displayed on his screen and surveyed the photo of the Dreamachine, a cylindrical sculpture with holes cut into its metallic sides, each varying in shape. At the base of the machine, a young woman with a brunette bob knelt down and leaned into the spinning sides, her nose just inches from the device. Her eyes were, of course, closed.

Jasper read bits and pieces of the article, skimming over a line about how the inventor envisioned the Dreamachine as *the successor to the television*. Had others in the sixties envisioned the same thing? Interesting, but also funny, he'd never heard of the thing until today. He didn't think many had heard of it, not to mention that the sixties, and the fads those years spawned, were light-years behind them.

Outside the edge of the article margin, glowed a distinctive arrow, like one you might see featured on a road sign, the yellow kind. Incidentally, yellow is the color the eye is drawn to the quickest. Jasper knew this—he knew a lot about color theory, actually—as color glued the eyes of online viewers to his web pages. Yellow gets people's attention, and this arrow had certainly gotten his. It pointed toward a hyperlink at the bottom of the page:

<u>SAMPLE</u>

He clicked on it, ignoring any implication that the use of yellow in this instance might have meant *caution*. He didn't care for the implication, not when it came to surfing the web.

The computer screen imploded to black, long enough for Jasper to wonder if he'd just downloaded a virus, before beginning to oscillate between white and black pages in such rapid succession that it created a stroboscopic effect. It was a simulated effect, not a glitch, but Jasper couldn't tell the difference. He had never been to a rave and he was prone to headaches; this was just about the last thing this man would ever think to want to subject his eyes to.

In spite of his predilections, he went ahead and leaned his face into it; it was as though part of him was being pulled into the pulsing screen. There was something comforting, or blanket-like, about it; it made his eyes warm.

Black.

White.

Black.

White.

Black.

And so on and so forth, but considerably faster than one could count or, eventually, even discern between shade—after a while, and it didn't take long, the effect appeared to become one unified pulsation, or signal of some sort.

Black.

WhiteBlack.

WhiteBlackWhite.

BlackWhiteBlateWhackiteBlWhctWeickBkWtiaeWBlieb cBiWetBclkWeBakcteittBhetiWhaBlate. The two tones just merged together.

If Jasper weren't so preoccupied, so magnetized, by the tractor-pull of these pulses, he might have noticed a vent in the ceiling above him, situated a few feet behind his head, as an almost imperceptible mist blew out of its aluminum slits. The thing was, in reality, he did notice it, but he just didn't seem to care. And because he didn't care, he would not even remember it later. *So be it*, he thought to himself, and then the thought was *gone*.

All that seemed to matter was the brightening and darkening of the pixels embedding themselves into his eyes.

CHAPTER TWO

PAIGE PULLED some items down from a medicine cabinet and approached her husband, who was sitting lethargically on the closed seat of the toilet. Hunched over, Jasper rolled up the sleeve of his wrinkle-resistant, blue polyester-blend shirt. As it happened, his spinal column and shirtsleeves were quite used to this position. Paige prepared a narrow syringe, inserting it into a bottle of insulin and extracting a full dose.

Jasper never really believed he had diabetes, the adult onset type; what do they say, denial is an antidote to woe? Or something to that effect. It's also one of the more dangerous kinds of antidotes, since he didn't do anything about *his problem* until he had already suffered irreparable vascular damage in his lower extremities. When Jasper hit his thirties, his pancreas simply stopped producing insulin, or at least enough of it to adequately control the glucose levels in his body. Like anybody, it stunned him: he ate right, exercised fairly regularly and kept his weight under control. His dad had it, when his dad was still around; he ended up dying from it. His mom had always said the disease was genetic.

The genes, the blessing and the curse—more often a curse as the years progressed. That's the way Jasper rationalized it. There was nothing he could do about it. His mom was dead, too. She turned an ankle and fell on the front steps of the house he grew up in, struck her head on the slate path, this not long after his father died. He remembered vividly how he helped his dad build that path when he was a kid; he even got to pick out the individual pieces of shaved sedimentary rock.

No siblings, no uncles, aunts, he was kind of alone on this earth, relatively speaking. He didn't really think about it much.

When he did think about it—when he felt alone—he knew that he really wasn't, because he shared a life with Paige, and for that he was grateful. Paige handed him the needle, its measured barrel loaded with the medication, and he injected it into his forearm, depleting the entirety of the fluid into his bloodstream.

*****

Later in the afternoon, Jasper sat in the waiting area of his general practitioner's office, reading a borrowed *New York Times*—not the *Arts & Leisure* section. He perused an article on the front page detailing President Rafferty's recent commitment to an overarching, and rather unprecedented, cut in defense spending. This was *The Age of Terror*, and the age had been monetized. It bored Jasper; in his mind, such a notion was nothing new.

He stopped reading somewhere in the middle of the patchwork of print and closed his eyes, as sleep had been scarce for him these days. It was just for a second, but it was a second of bliss.

He imagined himself back in the office, in his own knock-off Herman Miller chair, conversing with Cary at their cluttered desks, just the same way it happened before. The thing was, it was not like it happened before. It *was* before. He felt as though it was happening all over again; he could see it, he could feel the air blowing on him from the vent in the ceiling, he could smell Cary's sharp Ralph Lauren cologne—except everything was slowed down; it was dreamlike. But he wasn't dreaming, or daydreaming; he was awake, he was self-aware, and he was watching himself.

His perspective was tunneled again, a vignette of sorts isolating their heads, their mouths.

"Here's the kicker: he said that it allows viewers to see everything that can be seen, or has been seen, or will be seen," Cary said.

"Sounds like he's speaking of the 'collective unconscious,'" Jasper responded.

"He's speaking of... the future."

Their conversation continued; however, the images in Jasper's head began to disassemble, their words dribbling from their mouths and floating over discarded images that reassembled into an altogether different point of view: the back of that same pair of bright red stilettos.

"Yeah, I'm skeptical about the whole clairvoyance thing, myself, but imagine if it can unlock whatever it is that's up here..."

The stilettos climbed a curved wooden stairwell, ascending the final step, turning a corner and proceeding down the narrow corridor.

"I'd give it a spin around the block."

Jasper continued to stare blankly at the newspaper resting on his lap, staring with his eyes closed.

"Mr. Keepnews?"

Jasper's eyes darted up at the nurse standing over him. She was clutching a clipboard in one hand while holding the office door open with the other. She seemed much taller than she was, even a little imposing, probably because he had slid so deep into his seat. He folded the newspaper, tossed it onto the empty seat beside him and hobbled toward the nurse. When he sat for long stretches, he really started to notice the stiffness in his right leg; the sitting exacerbated it. He often had to hide his grimace when forced to stand up, and his reaction was no different here: an inviting smile, in a place where you can usually count on inviting the opposite.

Anyway, probably better to focus on the leg than this goddamn dream. There was nothing like a little pain to distract a person.

"Right this way, Mr. Keepnews," the nurse said.

"Thank you," Jasper replied, as he brushed past her into the modest corridors of the clinical wing.

Jasper sat on the edge of a paper-covered examination table as Dr. Blythe Desmarais held a tapered beam of light up to each of his eyes, dilating his restricted pupils. His eyes were a bit bloodshot, but no more than usual, mostly unnoticeable if a flashlight weren't inches from them. On the outside, Dr. Desmarais could easily be categorized as bohemian by modern standards, boasting a platinum nose-ring curled around a nostril and dirty-blonde hair. She was new at Dr. Aiden Michaelson, MD and Associates, which was not unusual; Dr. Michaelson employed a number of medical students, fulfilling internships and such, and every once in a while he staffed a doctor fresh out of medical school. Dr. Desmarais seemed to fall into the latter category, Jasper thought. Her sense of style may have been a bit scattershot, in his view—the view of someone whose wife picked out his clothes—but her hands were steady.

She brought the light down, slipping it into a pocket on the side of her loose-fitting light blue scrubs. Jasper locked eyes with her, smitten with what he saw around the sun-spots in his own, "Everything look alright?"

"Yes," she responded. "But I'm concerned about the sleeplessness, in light of your condition."

"I've been having these dreams."

"Is it a problem?"

"They're not exactly soothing; I guess they're more like nightmares... though I've had worse nightmares."

"What are the dreams about?"

"I'm not sure, exactly, but they always seem to take place in some foreign country, at least foreign to me—could be Europe, if I had to venture a guess—and they're extremely vivid, more so than I've ever experienced, which is the only reason I mention it. You know," Jasper chuckled, "my wife and I were supposed to go to Paris for our honeymoon, but we could never make it work with our schedules. Maybe that's haunting me, haunting my sub-conscious?"

"A lot of couples just wait for the right time." Dr. Desmarais continued to talk as she opened a wall cabinet, "There's no shame in that," which was filled with various medications and promotional pharmaceutical products. She pulled some of them down, scanning them briefly; but in no way should this swiftness be mistaken for neglect. Jasper could sense she cared, or that she at least knew what she was doing.

"I'm going to lower your insulin." Dr. Desmarais said.

"I'm getting better?"

"I don't want to jump to conclusions. I know that Dr. Michaelson had you on a regimented program, but I'd like to change it up a bit—as we get older, our body chemistries change. I'm also a proponent of more homeopathic, less intrusive, remedies." She smiled at him. "Let's take this one step at a time, if you're up for it, of course?"

He smiled right back, perhaps a little surprised, "I'm up for it."

"That's good to hear."

Jasper stood up, breathing with clear-cut relief and grabbing his jacket off the top of a stool, as Dr. Desmarais pulled a small bottle of medication from a multi-colored metal box.

"We have lots of free samples in the office. I'll give you a script for the refill—thought I'd save you some money."

"Thanks, Doctor."

Jasper was more than pleased, the hint of vibrato in his voice indicated as much, as she handed him the bottle. "Do you think these dreams mean anything?" he asked, curiously.

"It's not my area."

Jasper nodded, in as positive a way as he could.

"But I have read that recurring dreams can sometimes be an indication of a void your unconscious is seeking to fill—like the mind is on repeat until it finds what it's looking for." She chuckled, "That's my two cents on the subconscious, and believe me, it's probably only worth two cents."

"I'm sure it's worth a little more than that."

Dr. Desmarais walked him to the door and handed him her card. "Here's my number, should anything concern you." She put a hand on his shoulder as Jasper stepped out of the room. The small gesture was reassuring to Jasper, albeit a touch unprofessional if he really gave it some thought. But the way he saw it, in a business where saving humans was its bread and butter, being a human while doing so could only help, not hinder, the business model.

Jasper rolled into his office building's modest parking lot on his motorcycle, a used, and equally abused, Kawasaki Eliminator—Paige would never let him spend the kind of money he wanted to spend on a new Harley or vintage Indian bike. His ride had character, though. It was a cruiser, but considered a power cruiser, with a respectable amount of horsepower. It was designed to evoke the design of Kawasaki's Z1 drag bike. This model was, effectively, the watered-down suburban version—that's the way it was marketed.

Jasper parked the bike, climbed off its elongated quilted leather seat and booted out the kickstand. He grabbed his cane, which was tethered to the back of the stepped seat with a bungee cord. As he shuffled toward the front doors of the building, he shifted his weight sharply and his cane splintered down the middle. His knee buckled, the mass of his weight sending him hard to the ground. He winced, gritting his teeth, as his body lay outstretched atop the manicured grass.

He shook his head, as nonchalantly as possible, and struggled to suck in a breath for a second; the wind was knocked out of him and the muscles around his rib cage constricted like the jaws of a reptilian predator around its prey. He peered over at the bisected cane, lying across the bed of grass, as he clutched onto his lower leg.

With more than a modicum of effort, he managed to pull himself up without drawing attention. He began limping toward the office.

"What happened to your leg?" Cary asked.

Jasper slumped at his desk next to his co-worker, wrapping silver duct tape around his cane, jerry-rigging it back into functionality. The cane was never an aesthetic triumph to begin with.

"I don't mean to..."

Jasper put the cane aside, leaning it on the file cabinets behind him. "It's okay," he said, with a noticeable tinge of frustration. "I'm diabetic. I was aware of the symptoms;

just never got it checked out. I was a stubborn asshole." He forced a grin onto the bottom of his face. "Caught it in time to save the leg, but it paralyzed the muscles around my knee."

"Wow—"

The two men returned rather quickly to their work, diligently building websites for their clients. That's the good thing about conversations with co-workers in their line of business: there's never an awkward silence, or lull in repartee. Not when they can turn back to their computers and continue with the tasks at hand—there's never a shortage of work and the updates keep coming.

"How's your Dreamachine site going?" Jasper asked.

"Groovy, man. Grooooovy."

***

Inside Paige's brick-and-mortar Parchment Paper Books, Paige was in the middle of restocking the cluttered and dust-caked shelves. There was a low-hanging ventilation system, a series of metallic tubing reminiscent of veins, which featured a distressed patina on its outer surface, a shade of paint that was reminiscent of rust. The intent was to convey the feel of longstanding existence, giving it a vintage vibe, while paralleling the modern perception of books that is left largely unsaid: books are obsolete. The paper kind, that is. The simple act of reading as a leisure activity is becoming more and more of a chore for a lot of people, in the face of streaming video and news updates that limit the character count a writer, or any conscious being with a keyboard and a connection, can use to compose a written thought.

However, there is a movement toward—or perhaps more accurately, a regression to—Neo-Luddism, which embraces what some believe the modern world is leaving behind, both rapidly and haphazardly so. Although it's present, it's not so much an elitism that drives this dedication to past modes of communication—vinyl records, paperbound books, manual 35 millimeter film cameras—as it is an attempt to capitalize on nostalgia. Maybe that's why he kept his little notebook in his pocket, Jasper thought to himself.

There's a market for the past, and it's a lucrative one. While nostalgia is often viewed as the enemy of the future, it was certainly a catalyst for Parchment Paper Books and other shops like it. Why else would companies still be producing turntables and hardcover books, unnecessarily heavy accoutrements for a society that is becoming ever increasingly mobile?

The phone behind the counter began to ring. Paige swung by the counter, swooped up the phone and threw it against her ear. "Parchment..." A half-smile materialized on her face, "Hi honey," as she continued to toss books onto the shelves.

"Do you have any William S. Burroughs books at the shop?" Jasper asked, after the obligatory, *how're you doin'* patter.

Paige froze, halting the shelving of her books. "No. I don't carry them." She was silent for a moment, before probing further, "Why do you ask?"

"No reason in particular. Just felt like maybe reading some. Burroughs came up in a conversation at work."

"Really? Burroughs was a junkie, not a writer. He'd cut up, literally, 'cut-up,' other writers' words, then paste them together in a different order as if they were his own."

"Sounds like an interesting experiment."

"An experiment I wouldn't want to sit through five hundred pages of. Or subject my customers to."

She shoved the final grouping of books onto the shelf.

"I have to close up the shop tonight, so I'm gonna be home a little late. Call you later?"

Jasper hung up the phone and turned his attention once again to his computer. He quickly minimized his work—a spreadsheet of demographic data mined from the Midwestern United States—and opened his internet browser. In zero time at all, he was scrolling down a page entitled THE DREAMACHINE. Without prompting, blueprints for a *build-it-yourself* Dreamachine popped up on the page, along with a list of the basic materials for its construction:

- 36 x 36 (inches) black cardboard sheet
- 78rpm turntable
- Light bulb (opaque, 60W/100W) with cable

Jasper pulled the notebook from his pocket, flipped to the first empty page and began jotting down everything in front of him.

Back inside Parchment Books, Paige ambled down the first of the fiction aisles. She scanned through the "B" section of authors, arriving at several works by William S. Burroughs: *Naked Lunch, Nova Express,* and *The Ticket That Exploded.*

She removed all three books, without much care, and walked toward the back of the store.

CHAPTER THREE

J ASPER SHUFFLED through his local pharmacy clasping a basket, in which he carefully placed several household items: a wooden ruler; a razorblade; all-purpose glue; light bulbs. Searching along the bottom rack of a bank of adjustable shelves, he found the largest size of black poster board in stock. He grabbed a piece, folding it gently under his arm so as not to crease it before he returned home.

Jasper descended his basement stairs, a crinkly plastic bag of crafts firmly in his hand along with the poster board. He placed the bag on the floor and extracted each item with a pointed meticulousness and laid them onto the cushions of the couch, one alongside the other.

He placed the board on the floor, flattened the corners with the palms of his hands and hunched over it. He stretched open his notebook to a page on which he had copied a series of geometric shapes. He glanced at the book, then at the piece of cardboard, and began sketching the shapes.

These shapes were wedged between a plethora of research in Jasper's notebook—research he had dug up on the Dreamachine. The shapes are what Ian Sommerville and Brion Gysin, the inventors of the machine, referred to as Ishmaelite Archetypes. Jasper was intrigued to find that Sommerville was a computer programmer; he was a mathematician who served as William S. Burroughs' *systems advisor* and more than sometimes lover. In the early 60's, he developed a random sequence generator that Gysin, a Beat poet, used to develop his cut-up technique, which Burroughs borrowed and employed in his novels. Gysin—fellow novelist, reporter, promoter, provocateur, poet, painter, and self-proclaimed magician—was heavily influenced by Sufi philosophy (the Beats, generally speaking, were more than fascinated by Eastern, and Middle Eastern, religion) and devoted his aesthetic efforts to creating calligraphic works inspired by both Japanese and Arabic script.

The Dreamachine seemed the amalgamation of his life's work. It was described as "the first art object to be seen with the eyes closed." Sufism is considered a highly private, and possibly mystical, subdivision of Islam that has extended across oceans and into numerous cultures. Sufis practice Ihsan—worship in its most flawless state—as it was revealed to Muhammad: "Worship God as though you see Him, and if you cannot see Him, then indeed He sees you."

In religious Islamic art, geometric designs, floral designs and calligraphy are common. They generate impressions of never-ending repetition, which are meant to evoke the infinite character of God. The arabesque use of multiplicative polygons on the sides of the machine creates symmetrical patterns that project a plane of infinity in both directions.

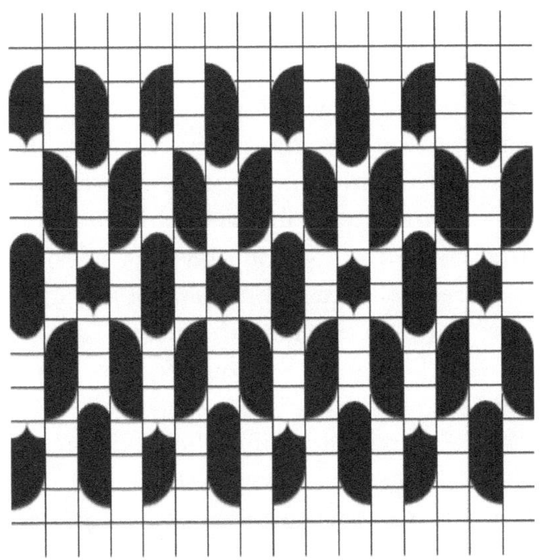

Jasper picked up the razor and began slicing into the series of shapes he had outlined on the poster board. He took his time, making sure his incisions were as precise as possible.

He thought about a connection he had made: Sommerville's background in mathematics and Gysin's penchant for Sufism coincided when considering the names of God in Islamic theology; expressly, how the words themselves correspond to numeric values. By way of example, if a specific name of God equals the value of twelve, then a believer will often repeat this name twelve times while he prays. The numeric value of each name of God is as important as the name itself for some followers, and the resulting repetitions of that name suggest the proper contemplation of God.

This is relevant in Islamic culture when worshippers consider what Allah's messenger was professed to have said: "Whoever correctly enumerates the names of God will enter paradise." There are ninety-nine names of Allah, each equaling a specific numeric value unto itself; comprehend them all, and that follower will be welcomed into the after-life.

Jasper always had an aversion to organized religion, and part of that aversion was the human element: he thought that to attempt to name the divine is to attempt to extrapolate a definition from an abstraction. How can something so finite as a word, with its limit of letters, of sound, of definition, describe the infinite? Sufi philosophy, on the other hand, disassociates itself from the name—the name as a word—and translates it into a number, which is arguably a step away from specificity toward abstraction.

According to this philosophy, the distinction is qualitative as well as numeric. The notion that a code, mathematical or otherwise, was behind the construction of faith was, quite possibly, akin to a kind of primitive computer programming. Jasper was a web designer, that was his title, but he also wrote his own code—one of few in his industry skilled at both tasks. So this notion, admittedly, did interest him: *religion as software for culture.* He who computes not only the quantitative values of the names of God, but also realizes the qualities, the virtues, of the name of God itself, will achieve Ihsan.

By way of a qualitative example, a name consisting of increments all valued at 1 is indicative of *unity, agreement, harmony*: 1 + 1 + 1 + 1 + 1 and so on. If the numeric value of a particular name is equal to 2, that may be indicative of *duality*—two sides to every coin, and the like.

As one contemplates these values, one cannot help but shape them, form them, visualize them. The Sufi proceeds to tilt his philosophy again, stepping one more increment away from the realm of the specific and into the ether of abstraction, by shaping the number, the meaning of the word, geometrically. The numeric value of 3 can be distilled into the visible: 3 points, a triangular form, a pyramid, and the like. This calls to mind the *enneagram*; a mandala of nine intersecting lines inside a circle, of which the triangle is the basis of its form, a shape that has been utilized in a variety of cultures, sects, organizations, including but not limited to the Jewish Religion, Orthodox Christianity, Anarchists, the Occult, etcetera. Mystics believe it is the key to revealing one's true self.

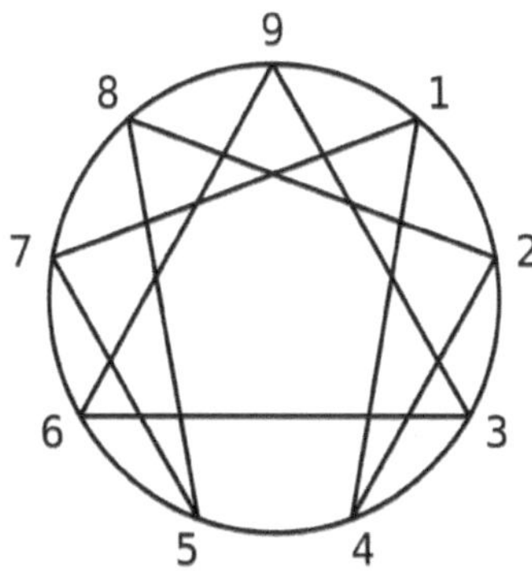

The drawing is based on a belief in the mystical properties of the numbers 3 and 7. The points are connected by two figures: one connects the number 1 to 4 to 2 to 8 to 5 to 7 and back to 1; the other connects 3, 6 and 9. The 142857 sequence is based on the fact that dividing 7 into 1 yields an infinite repetition of the sequence 142857. In fact, dividing 7 into any whole number that is not a multiple of 7 will yield the infinite repetition of the sequence 142857. Also, 142857 x 7 = 999999. And, of course, 1 divided by 3 yields an infinite sequence of threes. The triangle joining points 3, 6 and 9 links all the numbers on the circle divisible by 3.

The enneagram represents nine personality types. Sufi philosophy defines each of them by a *fundamental weakness* or *sin*:

The Perfectionist	One	Anger
The Philanthropist	Two	Pride
The Entertainer	Three	Deceit
The Romantic	Four	Envy
The Spectator	Five	Avarice
The Warrior	Six	Fear
The Gastronome	Seven	Gluttony
The Leader	Eight	Lust
The Mediator	Nine	Sloth

The repetition of numbers, of shapes, of modes of worship, of groupings of letters, is what the Sufis believe will bring them as close to the comprehension of God's infinite love on earth. It's really all about pattern; seeing God's presence in the patterns around us, patterns our imperfect human senses are largely unable, or unwilling, to recognize, whether it's through letters, numbers, shapes, or light: the light that illuminates all, the light that blinds, the light that brings things into focus, and it's through the repetition of light in which you will perceive God; and if you close your eyes, you will recognize the God inside yourself.

Jasper couldn't help but wonder about his fundamental weakness and to which category his personality belonged— this seemed of much greater importance to him than whether or not God existed, on this planet or anywhere else.

He unearthed a dusty record player from the corner of a cabinet. It was his father's. He didn't remember ever using the thing; he didn't remember his dad ever using it either. He took the poster board, which he had riddled with the five shapes, repeated in identical patterns according to Gysin's original design—

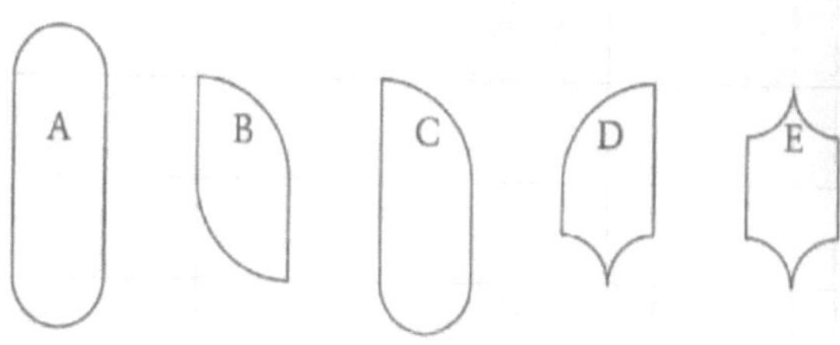

—and glued it together forming a large cylinder. He turned the tubular structure upright and attached it to the top of the turntable, adhering it to the platter with a glue gun he had been heating up.

He then took a malleable standing lamp and hung it precariously over the cylinder. He bent the top of the lamp, lowering the bulb into the tube and suspending it within its center.

He turned the lamp on, stepped back, and admired his work: the "Dreamachine." Well, his version of it.

Was that it? He guessed so and shut the rest of the lights off in the basement—only the glow of the bulb inside the cylinder remained. He walked toward the contraption, kneeling down in front of it as though it was some kind of altar. He squared his body up to it, straightening his back, and then he turned it on.

The turntable began to spin, the poster board rotating equidistantly around the bulb, flashing a matrix of light a-round the walls of the room. It took a few seconds to really get going, but soon enough the light brought to fruition a succession of shapes; this simple loop of paper and glue projected images of unending repetition—a mosaic of luminosity sculpted by the shapes Jasper had cut into it.

He brought his face in close, within an inch or two of the twirling cardboard. As the wind generated from its spinning wafted his hair back, he breathed in deeply and

closed his eyes, the surface of his lids splashed with a stro-
bing, and seemingly unending, luminescence.

***

Jasper jolted awake in his bed, coming face-to-face in the
middle of the night with what appeared in his nocturnal
grogginess to be a little girl standing at the foot of his
mattress, dressed in tattered overalls and her auburn hair
tied in pigtails.

He stared at her, and screamed, his scream involuntarily
morphing into a single word: "Paris!"

Rapidly blinking away the apparition, his wife roused;
this was clearly getting tiresome. "Go back to sleep," Paige
said.

Jasper, shaking himself more fully awake, caught his
breath—it felt as though he hadn't breathed for a few
minutes. He blinked his eyes, again, confused as to how he
even got into bed in the first place. He couldn't remember
at all.

Jasper slowly got up and lumbered into the bathroom.
He stared at himself in the mirror, blank as the expended
shell of a bullet. He looked into the discolored light fixture
suspended above the mirror. He began blinking at it. He
stopped, trying hard to think, however groggily. He looked
into the light and took his hand and waved it in front of his
face. Back and forth, like the shutter in a movie camera.
Faster. Then slightly faster. Creating a makeshift strobe-like
effect.

Suddenly, he fell backwards—

But instead of hitting the tile floor, he collapsed into his
bed, his head sinking into his orthopedic pillow. He blinked
once, maybe twice, and shut his eyes—

42

Jasper's mind, his body, or what he thought was his body, stood in his basement once again. The entire room was dark, except for the light of the Dreamachine. This was the same moment as before, when Jasper first used the machine. It was as though he was replaying the moment in his head, wherever his head was. He walked toward it, toward the device, kneeling down in front of it, in front of his altar.

He switched the turntable on. The machine began to spin, flashing a matrix of light around the room, his face almost touching the twirling cardboard.

Closing his eyes again, he found himself, or what he thought was himself—and a version of his point of view— inside a hotel hallway. In what appeared to be playing out in full, saturated, Technicolor clarity, the red stilettos, the pair he recognized from the fragments of his dreams, strode with purpose down the corridor, past a succession of identical doors. Each step was more certain, more precise, than the last; it was as though all the time spent studying the details of these feet and their footwear in the early morning hours of his slumber had paid off. The replaying and replaying and replaying of this vision had etched a groove into his subconscious mind, through which the needle of his synaptic phonograph was currently sliding.

The shoes came to their inevitable rest, pivoting toward the same door at the end of the hallway. The mystery woman opened the door, entered, and shut it closed behind her. The number on the outside of the door, also the same: 604.

But, somehow, something was different.

Hands, a pair of them, came into view, framed within whoever's point of view were snapping on lightly powdered surgical gloves and reaching for the door handle. One of the hands slid the magnetic strip of a card key through a reader in the handle and softly pushed the door open into the living room of a lavish hotel suite: plush Victorian furniture, ornate vases, replete with fresh orchids, and a glistening dark wood floor with an Oriental rug in the middle. The hands shut the door, silently locking it.

The man, whose point of view it was, slinked against a wall—Jasper presumed it was a *man*—brushing his back against the exposed brick and craning his head around the corner. He peeked into the master bedroom.

Inside, the mystery woman had just finished opening a narrow pair of French Windows and sauntered out onto a small balcony. The man entered the bedroom, walking with purpose toward the terrace.

The man reached for a curtain, a curtain that remained incongruously static—it was as though the climate that enshrouded the building was completely windless—and pushed it aside. The man approached the woman, oblivious to whatever nonexistent weather currently existed in the upper air, a woman who was gazing out at the skyline of a foreign, European city, quite possibly in Amsterdam, or France—rustic rooftops, triangular intersections, controlled waterways and the occasional modern building in the distance.

The woman turned, looking directly into the man's eyes.

This was what the man's eyes registered: she was gorgeous, and so was her flowing red hair. There was a splendor about her that was reminiscent of a 40's Hollywood starlet. She looked like Deborah Kerr, and this person, this woman who looked like Deborah Kerr, smiled at this man.

There was a moment, there's always a moment: the moment before.

The man seized the throat of this double of Deborah Kerr, squeezing it tautly, digging his nails into the narrow nape of her neck. Her eyes shot open wider than it seemed possible, as she very visibly choked, gurgling spittle from the depths of her esophagus. If it wasn't for the shock, and subsequent pain, which was delayed due to the shock, she might have noticed that she was being pushed farther and farther over the balustrade.

The hands held her, with a modicum of care and diligence, or so it appeared, until she looked back over her shoulder and realized what was actually happening to her. It was in this moment of recognition—her confirmation of the danger of this situation—that the man proceeded with what he was there to do, as though her confirmation of terror authorized him to proceed. He released her.

She tried to catch her breath, looking into the eyes of this man with a sort of desperate relief. If his mission was to scare her, the mission was an unadulterated success. The man, this perpetrator, bent down, fixing his gaze on her red stilettos. He removed her right shoe and cradled her bare foot, running a lone fingertip along the edge of her arch, a fingertip that was blotted with the blood from the back of her neck.

He smeared the blood, in a rather disinterested fashion, along the bottom of her foot. Then, in one swift motion, the man heaved the foot upwards, flipping the slender woman backwards over the balustrade, her heels tumbling over her head.

The man rose to his feet, peering over the balustrade, watching the woman plunge, screaming, to her death far below.

His eyes stared at her, as much as a camera might stare, since that was basically what this point of view, the eyes of this thing, was. It was a recording device that recorded a murder: forget what was recording the scene, that was irrelevant—it was being recorded to something, that was the relevant part; even if that something was as insubstantial as a dream.

The point of view tilted upwards, staring at the Europeanesque skyline. As the traffic screeched atop the street below, in an effort to avoid colliding with this mystery woman's prone and distorted body, a series of explosions began to erupt on a succession of roofs. From this vantage point, the blasts looked as real, or as fake, as a series of firecrackers spread just enough apart, but still attached to each other, dominoing into consecutive detonations.

The last to go was a large modern building, one that seemed to consist of seamless glass, gleaming from top to bottom, which flared into an enormous flaming torch in the middle of the city.

Jasper startled awake in his bathroom—

Though lying listlessly on the tile floor, he nearly snapped his own neck as he sprung awake this time. His stunted senses were in the midst of being drawn to a persistent knocking at the door.

"Jasper?" Paige shouted, knocking some more. "Jasper. Are you okay?"

Jasper roused, grabbing onto the edge of the sink and standing up. "I'm okay."

"Don't forget to take your insulin."

Jasper moved in increments, as if there were a delay in the signal from his brain to his limbs; he eventually removed the new bottle of insulin from his pocket. As the morning sun seeped through the windows, he stared at himself in the mirror, scrutinizing the outline of his gaunt face, his recessed cheeks wrapped around his jawbone like the latex gloves that were wrapped around the murderous hands from his dream. He may have been physically disheveled, that much was obvious to him and to whomever was unlucky enough to cross paths with him that day, but somehow things seemed clearer to him now.

The mist of ignorance was beginning to disperse. He filled a syringe with the insulin and delicately injected it into his flesh.

***

Jasper sauntered out the door and down the front steps of his house. Paige followed him surreptitiously—she neither said goodbye, nor acknowledged his departure, as she peered through a sliver of window next to the doorframe.

Jasper quickly bungeed his bag and cane to the back of his bike and kick-started the engine. He drove away as his wife watched him, sipping coffee from an insulated chrome thermos.

A moment later, Paige descended the basement stairs, flipped on the light, and noticed the new piece of furniture in the center of the room.

She stared at the Dreamachine.

CHAPTER FOUR

JASPER SLICED the wheels of his motorcycle through the street. He expertly navigated the pavement, whizzing past a line of trees, the sun flickering behind them; there was an abandon to his riding this morning that felt new to him. And he embraced it. He tilted his head up, the sky the only witness to his euphoria, and stared into the center of the sun. He was utterly captivated by the broken, rhythmic beams of light that fought their way through the foliage. He wanted nothing more in his life, nothing more at this moment in time, than to simply close his eyes and allow himself to be immersed inside a cocoon of shimmering warmth.

Just then: the ear-piercing beep of a car horn—

Jasper spun his head around, catching sight of the midsize sedan heading right toward him. He whipped the handlebars to the right and veered sharply back into his lane, his bike wobbling beneath him, the oncoming car just barely missing him. As he centered himself, along with his bike, he inhaled a succession of rapid, involuntary breaths, weaving his tongue around the curves of his teeth. Realizing he just avoided what could have been a major, if not fatal, motorcycle accident, he shook his head back and forth with the vigor of a man who couldn't be more upset with himself.

He continued to drive, trying to shake himself back into some semblance of normalcy. Beside the road loomed a large billboard: "TYMATROPE," over a picture of a statuesque doctor in a lab coat standing beside a smiling teenage girl on a swing hanging from a lush tree. Its tagline etched below the picture: "Tymatrope…Swing from the Tree Of Life." Jasper drove right past it.

His office cubicle felt like it had shrunk in size. Jasper sat inside its white plastic walls, staring out a nearby window down the hall. His eyes homed in on an unusually tall tree, a sycamore—they can grow up to a hundred feet, sometimes larger, and this one looked larger. He thought, for a minute, if he were at the company long enough, he might one day earn a cubicle that was even closer to the window, through which he could view this same tree. It was a small goal, but a goal nonetheless.

Suddenly, Jasper started to see something; something that was not in front of him, so to speak.

As he stared not at the sycamore, but into the sycamore, images began to appear in his mind like rapidly developed snapshots: The red stilettos; the "604" on the door; the woman who looked like Deborah Kerr plunging to her death; the skyline of a city erupting into flames. Each of them materializing like Polaroids being shaken inside the darkroom of his ocular cavities.

Then, a new one, a fresh neurograph, something he didn't remember from his dream began to develop: the view through the man's eyes became filled with a pair of hands rooting through the mystery woman's purse, his fingers pulling out a business card, embossed in gold flake:

LE RELAIS DE VIEUX PARIS
CYNTHIA J. ROBERTSON
CONCIERGE

Jasper twisted back toward his cubicle, pulled his chair snugly into his desk and woke up his computer—he realized he had not been getting much work done today. Even worse, he couldn't care less. He quickly typed "Le Relais de Vieux Paris" into a search engine. Results appeared, he glimpsed the first one: "Hotel Vieux Paris, 4 stars, latin quarter, paris charming …"

Jasper clicked on the link, which redirected him to the hotel's website. The page displayed a nostalgic image of an old hotel on the Seine River in Paris, France, and a superimposed portrait of a man, who had the look of a poet circa *The Birth of Cool*—thick, 50's-style, soda-bottle glasses, clutching a beat-to-shit book, an emphatic hand raised in the air. Jasper's eyes searched for the "about" section. He found it, clicked on it, scrolled around a bit, read a little, clicked again, scrolled some more, clicked, and after a moderate amount of buffering, the page produced an additional blurb about the hotel and its history:

Built in 1480, this historic hotel belonged to the Duc de Luynes and the Duc d'O and was once the dwelling place of Pierre Seguier, the true Marquis d'O. In the 1950's and 60's, American poets adopted the site and in the same movement created the "Beat Generation." Among them were Burroughs, Kerouac, Ginsberg, Corso...

Jasper leaned back in his chair, staring at the words on his screen: *Beat Generation.*

It didn't take him long to pick up the phone and start dialing—what the hell, he didn't pay the long distance charges. It rang and, eventually, a woman answered, speaking quite clearly in the French tongue, "Le Relais de Vieux Paris, appelez-vous pour une réservation?"

"Hello, yes, Bonjour, do you happen to speak English?"

"Oui. How may I help you, monsieur?"

Jasper paused for just a second; he hadn't thought this all the way through. "My wife and I are planning a trip—a second honeymoon, of sorts. I'm interested in reserving a room."

"Very good, sir."

"Is room 604 available?"

"Pardon?"

"I'd like to book room 604. If it's available."

"I'm sorry. This is not possible."

"What do you mean?"

"There is no room 604."

Jasper's eyes glazed over with confusion.

"We are planning a construction," she elaborated, "an extension of the top floor of the building. Perhaps, you have read this? It is possible there will be a room 604 next year, but right now there is not."

"Is this Cynthia Robertson?"

"Who?"

The hotel concierge giggled, slightly, like something was lost in translation, "Perhaps, monsieur, you have called the wrong hotel."

***

Cary stood at the front of a sleek conference room, a long frosted glass table before him like a diving board just begging to be jumped on, delivering a PowerPoint presentation to an eclectic group of clients sitting around it.

Grayson Emmett Lowell, a stout Southern Gentlemen in his late sixties with groomed mutton chops, sat at the opposite end of the table surrounded by cronies who all seemed to be leaning toward him. It was as though the man was magnetized. His presence was felt throughout the room, and not just by the paperclips; it was clear that Cary, who was helming this show, was directing the presentation solely toward him. And this man, Lowell, was most definitely not a bohemian.

"In W. Grey Walter's *The Living Brain*, he described a uniquely strange incident..." Cary explained, as his presentation played out on a state-of-the-art screen affixed to the wall, "...where a man in the audience of a cinema experienced a repeated impulse to strangle the person in the seat next to him."

Cary clicked a button on a small wireless remote in his hand and a video clip started to play. Film footage—it was digitized, but had the look of celluloid, anyway—of a man watching a silent movie in a cramped cinema came to life. The camera was positioned behind the man, as his eyes remained transfixed to the screen. More than that, really, he seemed hypnotized by the projection. After a few moments, the man abruptly turned to the patron sitting beside him, an unassuming elderly man in a herringbone newsboy hat, and stretched his arms out toward the other man's neck.

"As this man reached toward his fellow patron, and he looked away from the movie," Cary said, "he snapped out of it...and, eventually, turned his attention back to the flickering screen."

On the conference room screen, the man dropped his hands and turned his eyes back to the movie on the screen, as if nothing had happened.

"After a few minutes, he turned back to the man beside him and attempted to strangle him once again, just as he had done before, but again he came to before he could

follow through with it." Cary stopped the video. "And repeat, and repeat..."

He leaned over his laptop, manipulated a wireless mouse
and clicked to a slide of a large tree boasting bountiful
branches of leaves.

"It is interesting to consider the history of flicker..."

Cary's cell phone buzzed; its rather violent vibration
against glass interrupted his train of thought. He swiped it
off the table in front of him and looked at the screen. It
read: JASPER.

Cary looked back up at those sitting before him in the
room as his phone continued to buzz. He was preoccupied,
perhaps overly so—his clients noticed it, too. He glanced at
the phone once more. He looked at the time. It was just
about time for an intermission. He picked up another remote and pointed it at a wall. The overhead lights faded on,
illuminating the space.

"Let's take a break, shall we?"

Before he knew it, Cary was walking expeditiously toward the door and answering the phone, "Hello, Jasper."

Lowell hovered his substantial arm over the center of
the table and grabbed a glistening apple from a glass bowl.
He bit into the skin of the fruit as he watched Cary leave
the room.

On the other end of Cary's phone, Jasper sat in his
office, rather restlessly, continuing to peruse the website for
the Le Relais de Vieux Paris Hotel. "I really need to talk to
you," Jasper said in a hushed, but urgent, tone.

Cary shuffled away from the conference room, entered a
sterile hallway, "Sure, Jasper," and stepped up a flight of
stairs that brought him to an oversized steel-reinforced
door. He pulled an identification card from his pocket,
which was connected to his belt by a thin retractable wire,
and held the side of it against an electronic card-reader built

into the wall. Multiple locks in the wall disengaged and a green light built at the top of the doorframe blinked three times. Cary pushed the door open and walked through it—the outside of which was dressed unobtrusively shabby, as though intentionally so, concealing the hi-tech hallway inside—stepping onto the grounds of a vast apple orchard.

"I'm upstate at a presentation, but let's talk when I'm back in the office," Cary said into his phone, sounding simultaneously annoyed and eager to be of help.

"Thanks," Jasper replied, staring at the words on his computer screen: *Le Relais de Vieux Paris*.

***

In the confines of his office bathroom, Jasper splashed water on his face at the black marble triple sink while Cary lingered behind him. "The Beat Hotel is where Burroughs stayed, where he wrote, and experimented with his 'cut-up' technique," Cary said. He was in the midst of giving Jasper a kind of tutorial on the subject, while in an admittedly unusual venue—*Bathroom Beatniks 101*. Perhaps Cary had brought his presentation, or the demeanor he channeled while giving those types of things, back to the office with him.

Jasper glanced up at the reflection of his colleague through the mirror, "What I saw…it felt like it was going to happen. I understand this sounds ludicrous…but I felt it. I don't know how else to explain it."

"Who was this man? In the dream…the vision?"

"I don't know. I could see through his eyes, but it wasn't me—it was like I was someone else, like I had access to this person's body. My head feels jumbled. My thoughts feel…"

"Cut up?"

Jasper nodded.

54

"Burroughs," Cary said, "used to say, 'When you cut into the present, the future leaks out.'" He placed a hand on Jasper, cupping the top of his shoulder. "I gotta get back to this project, Jasper, I really do."

Just as Cary turned to leave, Jasper twisted back toward him, "Where was your presentation today?"

"These clients, they insist I come to them," Cary responded, smirking. "They're enormous pains-in-the-asses, there's no doubt about that."

"I know what you mean."

"Hey, almost forgot. I was sorting through some product samples this morning, cleaning house, and came across this super cool staff. It wasn't tagged. I left it at your desk. Figured you could use something to replace that bum cane of yours. It's just going to break again, might as well give this one a try. And did I mention it's super cool?"

"You don't know what cool is."

"I'm paid to know what cool is…or at least to sell what I think it is." Cary strode through the door, giving Jasper a tired but playful wink on his way out.

As the door shut, Jasper looked back into the mirror, zeroing in on his left forearm leaning on the top of the paper towel dispenser. He was stabilizing his fatigued body without actually realizing what he was doing, without realizing that he was barely able to stand upright.

Jasper approached his desk, finding the staff leaning on it. It was a long antique cane with a globular bronze handle. Engraved into the top of the handle were rather ornate Japanese characters: 古河

Jasper, almost unconsciously, began to rub his afflicted leg.

***

In his driveway at home, Jasper swung his leg off his motorcycle and extracted his new cane, which he had strapped smartly to the back. He limped his way toward the house, as he had done hundreds of times before—though it felt like thousands—weighing his gait into the cane, struggling with his mobility.

Jasper shuffled into his kitchen, lifting his nose into the air, giving the surroundings a vigorous sniff: Paige was at the stove sautéing a pair of chicken breasts in a simple blend of olive oil, garlic and rosemary. The sizzle in the pan and the odor it dispersed was a welcome invitation for Jasper. It almost made him forget how awful he was beginning to feel.

"Jesus…What happened to you?" Paige asked.

"I don't know." Jasper said, smiling, "It smells real good in here."

"Are you doing okay?" She paused cooking and walked straight up to him, scanning the sunken curves of his face.

"Feels like shocks are pulsing through my muscles." Jasper tried admirably to mask his trembling; sometimes shifting focus from a wounded sense to a hale and hearty one— in this case, smell—helped him manage discomfort and cope with the pain. "I'll be okay."

Paige noticed his cane, then looked him in his eyes: "Did you inject yourself this morning?"

"Yes." This was an answer he was used to delivering on autopilot. He hesitated a little, and then added, "The doctor prescribed me a lower dosage."

"Dr. Michaelson?"

"He was on vacation or something. There was a new doctor."

Paige waved a spatula dripping with vegetable oil at him. "Sit down, for God's sake." She turned back to the stove, and that was perfectly fine with both Jasper and his nose.

He sat down on a kitchen stool, leaning his cane against the edge of the center island.

"What's that contraption in the basement?" she asked.

"It's nothing…just an experiment."

"What are you trying to do with it?"

"It's an experiment with light, supposed to trigger lucid dreaming…at least from what I read. It's part of my research, for a new client at work."

"Did it work?" Paige smiled, the sarcasm vibrating from her lips.

"Not yet."

"You know, you could give yourself a seizure doing that—staring into blinking light. It's not safe."

Jasper: his visage was ghost-like.

"You are crazy if you think that thing will help you sleep."

"You're going to think I've gone completely insane, and maybe I have," Jasper snickered. "But I think someone's going to be murdered."

Paige didn't budge more than a millimeter; she just kept on cooking, attending to the domestic task at hand. The color started to come back to Jasper's face, declaring war on his paleness.

"A woman. At a hotel. In Paris. The room hasn't been built yet, but it will be. This woman will be thrown off the balcony to her death, just before the city of Paris is blown to fucking smithereens."

Paige couldn't help but laugh. "How can I respond to that?"

"It's this recurring dream I keep having—but I can honestly say I've never had a dream that felt this real."

"It's a goddamn nightmare, Jasper…not a dream!" Paige said with exasperation; she heard herself and began to tone it down. "They can shake people up, you'll get over it. You just need to get a decent night's sleep, watch your diet and stop drinking that cheap, terrible coffee you love to suck down. I want you to know that I made sure to buy organic chicken this time. You know that the antibiotics most farmers pump their chickens with can cause 'superbugs' in humans—superbugs—that are resistant to the kinds of antibiotics we're prescribed? Can you believe that? It's becoming more and more impossible to eat healthy in this day and age. I've even stocked up on my fresh spices from last weekend's farmer's market, so you're in good hands, my dear. The rosemary is out of this world good. You know, you should really listen to me more, I'm trying to do my best here." Paige laughed, perhaps a little too loudly, and then looked up, expectantly, at her husband, who hadn't moved a muscle.

Jasper, as though he wasn't even listening: "It's neither a nightmare, nor a dream."

Paige stopped her laughing.

"And I can't stop having it," Jasper said.

Paige placed her spatula down on a cutting board, and without turning, opened the utensil drawer next to her hip.

"It's like something inside me is telling me to stop it."

Jasper tried to chuckle, as if that's what he was supposed to do, but he couldn't. Even if he could, he would not have had the time to get one laugh out of his mouth before Paige pulled a handgun from the inside of the drawer—a compact son-of-a-bitch sporting a silencer and equipped with a laser sight.

She swung it toward him. Its laser etched a red circle into the sweat of Jasper's forehead.

Just as Paige readied her arm to shoot, Jasper flipped himself onto the Spanish-tile floor, grabbing his cane as he recovered his balance. A bullet ripped into the top of the granite, bits and pieces of rock splintering into the air around him, dusting the tops of his shoulders. Jasper planted his back against the far side of the island where only minutes ago Paige was, in all likelihood, chopping her much-touted rosemary and seasoning her organic breasts of chicken.

"Paige? What the hell are you doing?!"

She didn't answer, circling the island with the exactness of a soldier, her knees bent and weapon extended firmly in her hand. Jasper swung his legs around the counter, slamming the tops of his feet into her shins. She stumbled backwards, splattering a series of bullets haphazardly into the floor.

Jasper leapt to his feet. Gripping his cane tightly, he swung it at Paige, batting the gun from her hand. As the weapon tumbled to the floor, she threw a swift punch at him before it even made it to the ground. Jasper blocked the slug with the cane. She threw two successive punches, and then wound her body up for a roundhouse kick.

Jasper caught her foot in midair, with near-expert precision, and spun her around in the opposite direction.

As she regained her center of balance, facing her husband, Jasper raised his cane, pointing the globular bronze handle at her. It was all she could see before he swiftly jabbed it at her. The round metal piece detached from the rod, bursting out of the top, a thick metal chain attached to the bottom of it. It struck Paige straight in the face—her left upper cheek, the zygomatic bone, to be exact. The bronze handle hung from the foot and a half of chain like a medieval morning star.

Paige froze; she was stunned, her cheekbone having been broken into three parts, her body arresting itself in a helpless state of physical shock. It was startling that she was still standing.

Jasper swung the cane, wrapping the chain around the circumference of Paige's neck, cutting off the air to her windpipe, and paralyzing her larynx. The weight of the ball locked the chain into place. Her hands reflexively snapped to her neck, digging her fingers between the coarse links and her persecuted flesh, trying, desperately, to pull the chain away from her.

Jasper gazed at her with eyes as dead black as a shark's eyes. She summoned her adrenaline and rushed toward him, loosening the chain in a last ditch effort to get it off her neck. Jasper tightened the chain, halting her advance and dropping Paige summarily to her knees.

She gasped for a breath, her face flushed and bloated. Then she toppled onto her back, the sharp edges of her shoulder blades digging into the immovable surface of the floor.

Jasper stood over the writhing body below him. He brought his right foot down onto her neck, pressing the chain deeper into her throat, puncturing her previously un-blemished skin. She feebly ran her hands up his leg, grab-bing a hold of his knee—which was fully extended—the strength that streamed through his revitalized appendage was intimidating.

Her eyes widened as Jasper tensed his muscles and jerked the chain, breaking her neck instantly.

A stillness unlike anything he had ever experienced fell over the room. He studied Paige's corpse, astonished by what he'd done; his emotions had not quite caught up with his physical metamorphosis.

He choked back the first influx of tears, as he began to drown in a flash flood of overwhelming sorrow, "Paige?"

The tears began to flow: Jasper was inconsolable.

He lingered, wiping at his tears. The muscles beneath his cheeks trembled ever so slightly, as the rest of his body remained motionless. It was impossible for him to make sense of what had happened, what he had done—but the one thing he did know for certain, in this moment, was that he could not continue to just stand there over his wife's corpse.

He realized this the millisecond before he ran from the room, his limbs and corresponding parts moving like a well-oiled machine.

CHAPTER FIVE

BOOKS LINED the walls—their timeworn spines perhaps indicative of a penchant for collecting—a gigantic globe was situated in the corner and matching brown leather couches sat atop a blood-red carpet. Hiroshi Ito stood in the center of the room, an ostensibly Americanized Japanese man in his mid-fifties with a Lincoln beard, groomed tidily despite the noticeable razor burn where his neck met his collar; debonair pinstripes layered over a ruthless savage, there was no doubt.

His fellow agents knew very little about the man—and they got the feeling it was for their good, not his. He was as closed a book as the ones on his shelves.

Ito reached toward a bookshelf and carefully extracted the sore thumb of the room: a rectangular sandblasted metal box. He opened it and pulled out a narrow flashlight-esque gadget from its molded velvet womb—the velvet was a pale purple, not quite a uterine pink. Judging from the small size of the instrument, the box that contained it seemed unnecessarily cumbersome. Ito held the device in the palm of his hand, as if he were testing its weight, scrutinizing it with a mixture of reverence and apprehension.

Another man entered in a hurry—if a demeanor could ooze *lackey*, this man's demeanor did just that. "Agent Ito," the man said.

Ito turned sharply towards this man, Agent Graham Simmons, as he placed the device back into its container. He shut the box closed, put it back where it came from, and looked at Simmons as though he were about to open another one, an altogether larger one, that was exponentially more difficult to lose on the shelf.

The truth was, Hiroshi Ito had been waiting for this specific moment to arrive for a very long time.

***

Jasper flew down the street on his motorcycle, the wind wiping away any secretion that resembled tears from his face. It was just him and the road. He bent his torso close to his vehicle as if to make sure he felt every imperfection in the pavement, so he didn't have to feel anything else.

In the Keepnews foyer, there was a moment of near tranquility before the front door was kicked in, its hinges snapping off the frame. A throng of agents in per-the-job black suits and requisite rubber earpieces poured into the heart of the house. Each and every one of their guns were drawn; they performed a rapid and methodic room-to-room, clearing the physical premises in anticipation of a threat, or a man down.

Agent Ito stepped into the home; any quaintness that once existed within these domestic walls had become an irrelevant, and rather indistinct, memory. It was more like it never existed at all.

He walked through the front hall into the kitchen. Two agents hovered over Paige; one had two fingers planted on her bloodied neck. The other peered up at Ito as he approached, shaking his head at the dismal surroundings.

"Leave me," Ito ordered.

The two agents promptly left as Ito knelt beside Paige's dead body. He brushed the strands of hair away from her eyes and took her hand into his own. He traced the threadlike lines in her palm with his eyes, working his way up from the top of her wrist to the bottoms of her fingers. His eyes stopped at her wedding ring, a brushed gold band adorned sparingly with pint-sized diamonds and sapphires. He stared at the ring as he removed the modest piece of jewelry from her finger—his semblance of calm transforming into rage; his fury instantaneous, as if switched on by some electrical circuit.

"You failed me," Ito whispered.

Ito pitched the ring across the room; it hit the far wall, tumbling onto a side table before coming to a teetering rest on the floor.

***

Inside the high-ceilinged local public library, Jasper walked to the far end of the room and then hunkered down at a desktop computer in what appeared to be a patron-free corner. The library was barely populated at this hour. He briefly glanced at his peripheral surroundings as he opened an internet search engine and began typing into it:

CYNTHIA J. ROBERTSON

A seemingly endless list of links materialized. Jasper, his right leg pumping anxiously, scoped the area around him—it was the first time he really looked. He noticed a diminutive teenaged girl at a computer near him wasting time on the web, surfing some kind of social networking site. He scooted his chair back and leaned over her shoulder, catching sight of the address: www.socialbugg.com

He typed in "socialbugg" and brought the website's homepage up on his screen and typed Cynthia's name into it: another enormous list of name results. He clicked the "advanced search" option and added the keyword: "Paris." The list did shorten a bit, but it was still extensive; however, beside each name was the gift of a thumbnail picture. There were a few Cynthia Robertsons listed as residing in Paris, France; none of their pictures matched the woman from his dream.

He scrolled through several more pages, filtering multiple variations of "Paris" as a designation. Then it hit him like a dart in the back of the neck. "Paris..." he realized, he thought to himself: it's a name, not a place.

He kept on searching, then stumbled upon the profile: *Paris; 18 yrs old; San Francisco, CA.* Its corresponding photo consisted of an enticing close-up of the small of this woman's back, the skin of which boasted the greenish-black tattooed ink of a Japanese phrase.

Jasper just stared at it; he was no expert in foreign languages, especially those of the East. But he was sure this was Japanese. He was sure because he had seen this phrase before: he grabbed his cane and ran a hand over the handle—engraved into the bronze, were the same Japanese characters.

He turned back to the computer, clicked on the picture, opening thumbnail links to the woman's personal photo albums. Images of Paris in poses suggestive of a career in modeling, or at least the pursuit of one, populated the screen; they were professional-looking enough, well lit, but in an age when everybody snaps photos of themselves and posts them on a daily, if not hourly, basis, it was tough to tell whether these pictures were indicative of anything aside from a fondness for breaking men's hearts.

Jasper quickly scanned through the rest of the photos, bringing the cursor over one entitled: "Family." He clicked on the word and a single photo popped up: Paris as a little girl, no more than ten or eleven, who looked similar to the girl Jasper had envisioned earlier, in his somnambulant state, at the foot of his bed. In this particular image, she wasn't alone; she was flanked by a woman and a man—a couple who were presumably her parents, if his understanding of the traditional family portrait and how such a photograph is customarily shot is any precedent. The woman was the same woman from Jasper's dream, the one to whom the business card of "Cynthia Robertson" belonged, and the man was… Jasper.

Jasper stared at himself—his face was blank, as blank as his recollection.

***

In the lot of Jasper's doctor's office, Dr. Blythe Desmarais climbed out of her sleek BMW coupe, swatting its door closed and chirping its anti-theft alarm. As she approached the modest medical facility—its look was reminiscent of one of those hourly roadside motels, the two-floored sort with the beige stucco—she snapped open her purse and dropped her keys into it, but they missed, falling to the ground.

As Blythe squatted down to retrieve them, and then stood back up, she came face-to-face with Jasper standing in front of her.

"Jesus," Blythe blurted. "Mr. Keepnews?" She was startled; there was no hiding that. "Are you all right?"

66

Jasper pulled Paige's handgun halfway out of his jacket, brandishing its butt into her eyeline. His hand was visibly shaking. "I need your help." He was not threatening her so much as pleading.

Blythe sensed this feeling, which could have very well been a hint of desperation, or even confusion; she saw it clearly in his eyes.

Moments later, Blythe's BMW sped along the freeway, cruising under a large road sign: I-5 South. Blythe was doing the driving. Jasper was next to her in the passenger seat, watching her drive, as best as he could focus his attention in his stunned state.

"Where are we going?" Blythe wondered.

"Keep driving." He shifted in his seat, turning his body toward her. "Who do you work for?"

"What do you mean?" Blythe asked, cocking her head slightly. She was at a loss for words.

The strip of road ahead was barren; until another vehicle, a dark SUV wrapped in tinted windows, pulled up behind them. Jasper began to unconsciously rub his knee with his thumb and forefinger. He turned to the side-view mirror, noticing the rapidly approaching truck. He pulled out Paige's silenced .9mm pistol—it was next to Blythe's head in a millisecond.

Blythe jumped with fright, "Oh my God! Jasper," generating sound past a substantial lump in her throat, "what are you doing?!"

"Who are you?"

"You know who I am!"

He raised his voice: "The insulin you prescribed me— you *gave* me—it wasn't insulin. It was something else. What the fuck was it?!"

As he kept the barrel of the gun flush against her temple, he glanced behind him through the rear window at the
trailing truck.

"I can explain," she said.

Jasper rolled down his passenger door window. The
sound of the oncoming engine roared as the SUV squared
up next to him.

"What's going on?!" Blythe asked, glancing at the SUV
through the open window.

The SUV was close enough to discern two men in its
front seats wearing black ski masks and wielding compact
submachine guns. Their windows were already open and
their automatic weapons poised: they began to pepper the
side of Blythe's car with bullets.

Blythe barely kept her hands on the wheel as she ducked
her head under the lip of the dash. Jasper rolled himself
backwards into the backseat. He grabbed his staff, pulling it
toward him.

"Open the sunroof," Jasper ordered.

Blythe, stricken with panic, was literally unable to move.

"Do it NOW!"

She did as she was told, engaging the roof switch and
popping her head up just enough to give her some line of
vision on the road. Jasper bolted upright, projecting his
upper body through the sunroof, along with his staff.

The SUV hugged the right side of Blythe's car, remaining as parallel to it as possible. As their pursuers took
aim, Jasper snapped his staff at the truck—the metal ball
burst haphazardly from the top, swinging from its chain
and smashing into the center of the windshield like a
scaled-down wrecking ball.

The masked men recoiled from the splintering glass, a
tidal wave of shards crashing into their faces.

Jasper whipped the staff again, training the ball toward the driver's side and hooking its chain around the steering wheel. He shifted his body weight back, yanking the chain with enough force to engage the wheel and begin turning the SUV. He tossed the staff to the side of the road and plunged back down into the front seat, hip-to-hip with Blythe, jamming his foot onto her foot, squeezing down on the brakes. He slowed her car down just enough to avoid the SUV as it cut to the left—the out-of-control truck roared past them, barely avoiding a bone-crushing collision.

The SUV turned so sharply, the angle so extreme, that it flipped over, several times, its metal body scraping against the pavement as the wreck tumbled over the divider and lodged itself in a ditch along the opposite side of the road.

Jasper passed the wreckage, monitoring the carnage in the mirror as he finally brought Blythe's car to a stop.

He put the car into reverse and maneuvered it carefully back toward the smoking debris. He stopped the car within fifteen feet and hopped out. With his gun drawn, he sidestepped the divider, circling the SUV. The rear door opened and two masked men stumbled out coughing like bees being smoked out of their hive. Jasper grabbed the man closest to him and ran him into the ground face first, knocking him out cold. He spotted the other man running up behind him, raising his submachine gun. Jasper pivoted, grabbed hold of the barrel, and pulled it forward as the man frantically pulled the trigger. Jasper pointed the weapon, along with the wrath of ammunition it was spitting out, toward the unconscious man on the ground—he began convulsing as he was riddled with what no doubt felt like an endless number of bullets—bullets that had likely reached a temperature of over 300 degrees Fahrenheit apiece, bullets that were now irreversibly liquefying this dying person's insides, accelerating the process of physical decomposition faster than anything this man, this transgressor, may have ever imagined possible.

Jasper ripped the gun from the triggerman and snapped its butt into his face, upending his nose deep into his cranial real estate. Blood erupted from his attacker's face like a bottomless volcano as his body melted to the ground.

Shuffling to the driver's side window of the truck, Jasper assessed the condition of the driver. It was immediately obvious that he was dead, the side of his head impaled by a piece of the windshield. As Jasper dragged the body of the driver out through the window, another masked man crawled surreptitiously out of the shattered rear passenger side window.

Jasper rolled up the driver's mask, revealing the face of Agent Simmons. As he looked Simmons over, Jasper's eyes darted to a shadow snaking its way along the pockmarked ground. Before he could twist himself around, he heard a gunshot ring out—

The other masked man, the shadow's owner, collapsed to the ground at the base of Jasper's feet, blood splattering around his newly minted corpse. As the body fell, it revealed the silhouette of a woman. It was Blythe, a gun gripped tightly in her hand as if it were part of her anatomical structure.

She holstered the pistol with an air of authority, looking at Jasper soberly. "We need to get out of here," she said.

Jasper nodded and turned back toward the car without thinking twice; but first, he headed across the street to retrieve his staff.

***

Blythe's car sat covertly underneath a massive bridge in an industrial part of Nowheresville, the sky as steel gray as the bridge. Blythe handed a tablet to Jasper inside the vehicle.

"Sugar water," she said.

Jasper glared at her.

"It wasn't insulin. Sugar water is all it was. You were never prescribed insulin, not from Doctor Michaelson, not from anybody."

"Well, isn't that ironic …" he mumbled, as he perused an open folder of pictures on the tablet. He swiped through photos of his house, office, Paige, his entire life—all of it was displayed in front of him.

"What is this? What the hell is happening to me?!"

He threw the tablet to the floor.

"Your life, as you've known it, is a simulation—a mock-up orchestrated by the D.I.C.," Blythe said.

"D.I.C.?"

"Department of Information Control."

Jasper picked the device back up and continued to flip through the electronic dossier, in a simultaneous effort to ignore and dig deeper. He came across an exhaustive PDF list of names; the names of his co-workers. Blythe observed him as he absorbed the names.

"The organization you've been employed by for the past twelve years."

"Employee?" Jasper responded. "You make this department, or whatever it is, sound like some fucking fast food restaurant."

"You're an agent, put on stasis…"

Jasper could not help but release a sputtering sigh, "Until?"

"Until they have a need for you."

Jasper kept swiping through the digital pages; he was compelled to, he would be hard-pressed to stop if he tried.

He did pause, however, when he reached the biography of Cary Bryan. While he was taken aback, there was a part of him, he thought, that was expecting this particular page from the start.

"I don't understand. This is everybody I work with. I'm just a web designer and sometimes computer programmer; I punch in, punch out." He swallowed hard. "It's my job."

"They're all agents assigned to watch you—that is their job," Blythe struggled with delivering this news, "reinforcing the construct of your life, working in conjunction with the designated simulation."

"Simulation?"

Even if there was nothing inside him, not a single cell, that could have predicted this, Jasper remained unable to reconcile the outrageous degree of his blindness. This organization, this *department*, was involved in signing, sealing and delivering an entirely different life to his doorstep, a life he had no idea existed. He felt like he better pretend to believe there was something inside of him that knew, well, *something*—because a hoodwink of this magnitude was completely unacceptable to him; he simply couldn't fathom it, his mind couldn't comprehend it, and surmised that he may not be able to live with himself, whoever that self ultimately was, if his self were a victim of such an existential fraud.

He put the tablet on the dashboard, shoving it into the crevice between the dash and the glass of the windshield. He opened the door and climbed out of the car. He walked to the front of the vehicle, bent his knees and draped his back onto the hood. The blood rushed to the back of his head as he breathed in a pocket of polluted air. He stared vacantly at the underbelly of the bridge, listening to the engines of cars zooming along the highway, as he closed his eyes—

His consciousness began to slip, as though it were skating on ice. A variation of his recurring dream washed over him, washed over his consciousness—

The mystery woman, Cynthia Robertson, strolled onto the balcony. The eyes of her murderer approached as she gazed at the Parisian skyline. Cynthia twisted around, looking directly into those eyes. Her gorgeous red hair flowing in the wind. She smiled, lovingly, longingly, lasciviously—

A voice from far off echoed: "Jasper …"

It was Blythe's voice, retrieving Jasper from of his reverie. He slowly opened his eyes to find Blythe sitting next to him on the edge of the car hood, leaning her body over his. Jasper began to convulse, unable to control the random and seemingly rogue muscles stretching throughout his body that were trembling in perfect sync with his increasingly unstable emotions.

"I killed my wife." He brought his hands to his face, weeping uncontrollably. "I killed my fucking wife."

Blythe wrapped her arm around him, which he grabbed, wrapping his arms around her forearm and bringing his face close to hers. Blythe, breathing heavily, "I'm sorry..." In an attempt to calm him, she said, "The woman you killed, Paige, she was not your wife."

He loosened her arm from his grip.

"You meant nothing to her—you were nothing more than a mark in a long-term con."

He winced at the mention of his wife; specifically, the newly perceived meaninglessness of her role in his life.

"Trust me when I tell you that."

"How can I possibly trust you?" Jasper asked.

"The name of your real wife is Cynthia Robertson. But that's all we know. The identities of your family members are sealed, per agency protocol."

Jasper wiped the tears from his cheeks, galvanized by the mention of Cynthia's name. He hopped off the hood and staggered away from the car.

"I'm one of a number of D.I.C. agents who 'disagree' with the agency," Blythe said, and then continued, "We have been compiling information on conditioning practices—practices the department has been developing, and implementing, since its inception in the mid-60's."

Jasper stopped in his tracks, turning around to face her. "Human conditioning…" he mumbled.

"The 'Human Programme.'"

Blythe pushed herself off the car, hopping to the ground and leaning a hand against its driver's side door.

More memories washed over Jasper like a slideshow, the first a flash of his morning routine: sitting on the toilet while his wife, Paige, crouched beside him. "*The insulin you've been injecting—it's a drug that was developed by the D.I.C.*" As these cerebral snapshots appeared and disappeared, Blythe's words reverberated in the air, as though they were the soundtrack to Jasper's memories. Paige prepared a syringe and injected Jasper in the leg with what appeared to be insulin. "*…as a correlate to various triggers written into the narrative of your simulation.*" Jasper looked up at his wife; in hindsight, he might have pleaded with those eyes, endeavoring to connect to whatever humanity lied beyond them, from whatever humanity lied beyond his own. "*It operates as a conduit to the brain.*" Paige smiled dutifully at her husband: Jasper, her mission in life.

Jasper struggled with this information, statistics that were superimposed over his postscript trance, as he meandered back to the car.

"It streamlines the conditioning," Blythe explained to him. "The triggers activate it, and your mind reboots itself."

"Triggers?"

"Patterns. Patterns of light."

Things were starting to become clearer to Jasper, or at minimum the blindness caused by his emotions was now beginning to assuage.

"It can also be used to anesthetize the nervous system. A mixture of MAO inhibitors and experimental compounds…when taken in higher doses, it can cause severe muscle cramping and paralysis."

Jasper lifted his leg, planting the bottom of his foot on the hood of the car and rolling up his pant leg.

"It keeps you under control."

Jasper lowered his hand to his knee, massaging it with his fingers. He traced the circumference of his kneecap with his fingertips, pressing into the tissue around it as though he was trying to get under it.

His mind was assaulted, once again, with the image of Cynthia Robertson falling backwards from the balcony, in what seemed like a subconscious form of slow motion, her red hair fluttering in front her face—covering her mouth as she screamed, before she hit the Paris pavement. The image was burnt into his memories, into his mind, into his brain matter, like a sunspot burnt into his retina.

Jasper rolled his pant leg back down over his knee. "What have I been conditioned to do?" he asked.

"Can't you guess?"

Jasper just blinked at her; how does someone in this situation even begin to venture a guess?

"You are conditioned to kill."

Blythe squared up to him, taking his hand in a facile attempt to connect—she weaved her fingers through his.

"This life you're living…our knowledge of it is the extent of our intelligence. You are the key to exposing this. Only you know what they did to you, what happened, and maybe, what's going to happen."

Jasper looked up at her, tilting his head at her. She reached out, placing her hand on the side of his head: "The key is in there."

Jasper was awake for the first time, having been asleep for far too long.

CHAPTER SIX

TANGERINE SUNBEAMS were just beginning to rise as a chopper landed on the rooftop helipad of a gargantuan office building. The building itself eclipsed the others around it; it was a monolith. The sound of the fluttering helicopter blades echoed off the surface of the steel roof, bouncing into the atmosphere, acting as a sonic cushion upon which Ito stepped as he disembarked the aircraft.

Ito glanced into the blinding light of the horizon before being ushered into a nearby stairwell by the cluster of security that awaited him. This was D.I.C. Headquarters; Los Angeles, California.

Ito sat patiently across from The Director, a large, bald man with a hunch to his spine that was almost certainly a result of his years in this position. He did not look *at* Ito so much as he looked *into* him, and he was looking for answers, answers that were difficult to ascertain, no matter how simple the questions and their corresponding answers may have seemed.

"The package is in the open…and on the move," Ito said, matter-of-factly.

This information was greeted with immediate, and pervasive, silence. There were two guards posted in the room, manning its two windowless corners—their lack of body language was more expressive than the Director's.

"But there's an even greater complication," Ito continued. "There's been a breach. We have confirmation that a number of agents have broken from the division."

"What kind of number?"

Ito didn't respond; he didn't plan to.

"Jesus," The Director muttered.

"It appears they have gone into business for themselves."

The Director shifted his weight away from Ito, twisting uncomfortably in his patent leather chair—he massaged its chrome arms as though he were revving the engine of a motorcycle.

"Shut it down. Shut it down as quickly and quietly as you can."

"Yes, sir," Ito nodded. He had to agree with his boss, even if he realized the solution to this problem was far more complicated than The Director or any of his desk agents could imagine.

"What is it that they want?" The Director asked, at the brink of exasperation.

"My guess is they want what Jasper's looking for," Ito responded, tilting his head at his superior: "Paris."

Not long thereafter, teams of Special Operations Personnel poured out of the rear entrance to the building. The men, and presumably women—though gender was impossible to discern—were all dressed in the same virtual SWAT attire, which included custom-made bulletproof vests and riffs on riot gear helmets, and each armed with an automatic assault rifle equipped with a laser scope. These heavily-metaled soldiers filed into a fleet of black vans.

Ito hopped off the loading dock, dressed in a similar fashion and speaking into a headset that hugged his jawline: "First team en route." He climbed into the passenger side of the lead van as it shifted into gear and accelerated into the street and down the northwest block.

The other vans followed the leader.

***

Blythe found herself behind the wheel of her car, relieved of her role as *carjacking victim*—her role in Jasper's story had become exponentially more complicated, perhaps even vital, in his mind. She cruised steadily atop the obsidian asphalt of the Interstate 5. She passed a sign: SAN FRAN-CISCO.

Jasper's notebook rested on the center console. It was bent open to a page scribbled with information on Paris he found on socialbugg.com. "You think she's your daughter?" Blythe asked, glancing at the notebook.

"I don't know," Jasper responded, awkwardly hunched over a laptop in the passenger seat. He accessed the internet via the hotspot on Blythe's phone, hacking into the San Francisco Department of Motor Vehicles' server with the help and guidance of his *doctor*. Or was she his *handler* now? Jasper couldn't be sure, but he was sure that he couldn't be sure, and he didn't have anybody else to be even partially sure about right now. Best to focus on the task at hand: the government server he was attempting to penetrate. It was supposed to be secure, but it was the DMV—if anything could be hacked, it was the bureaucratic clusterfuck that was the Department of Motor Vehicles. "But it's a distinct possibility," Jasper continued, "and if I can find her, that means I'm one step closer to finding Cynthia."

Blythe wanted to nod, to agree with him, but thought better of it. It might have given him false hope. "I had an uncle who was a research analyst for the government," she said.

A rectangular box popped up on Jasper's computer screen. "Password?"

"I-25-PEP-8912." Blythe responded, and then chuckled, "He went through a period where he conducted weekly optical experiments and was instrumental in the creation of early retinal ID scanners. He was obsessed with how the retina perceives visual information."

After the state-run website accepted the password, without much electronic resistance, a search engine appeared on screen. Jasper typed: "PARIS ROBERTSON."

"One weekend he brought me his 'upside-down' glasses. Our retina reads everything backwards—it inverts the image. These glasses used two lenses for each eye, which would reverse the light entering and exiting the glass."

Jasper listened to Blythe speak, but he maintained a steely focus on the screen as the engine searched for results.

"My uncle let me wear them around the house."

"Doesn't sound very safe," Jasper responded.

"He was the expert, what did I know? I was eight. When I put the glasses on, everything was upside-down. The whole world. But after I wore them the whole weekend, my brain adapted to it, correcting the image." There was a wisp of nostalgia in the words that left her mouth. "It turned everything back the way it was. Right-side up."

The search engine continued its searching; the extended buffering seemed to mimic the length of the lines in the actual DMV, which only added to Jasper's frustration.

"Maybe our brains only allow us to see what we want to see," Blythe said.

Several designations finally appeared on screen that included the first name "Paris," the origins of which were peppered throughout the greater San Francisco area.

"There appear to be three Paris's in San Francisco," Jasper said.

He scanned the images of their driver's licenses: one was a man, the other an elderly woman, and the last was PARIS CHILDRESS, who was listed as being eighteen years of age. Jasper felt like smiling, though no bright moment in this spectrum of darkness could justify the gesture—

"I found her."

He stared intently at her ID picture as Blythe's ears perked up.

"How can you tell?"

"I suppose a father can just tell." He let a little laugh seep out. "I can't believe I said that."

He clicked Paris's hyperlinked name, prompting another bout of buffering, before bringing up her address: 128 Clayton Street, San Francisco, CA 94117. As he twisted his torso toward Blythe, she did notice the hint of a smile. She nodded her head at him; it was a somewhat indifferent nod, the tone of which implied a touch of cautious encouragement.

***

Blythe's car traversed Haight-Ashbury, the famous—or infamous, depending which political wing one leans to— artery of bygone hippiedom. She cruised past the Piedmont Boutique, where giant fishnetted legs equipped with red stiletto shoes protruded provocatively out over the storefront. The sign above it boasted: *The Ultimate Source for Custom Fashions, Lingerie, Fetish Wear, Hosiery, Accessories, the Most Unique of Jewelry, Earrings, Necklaces, Bracelets, Rings, Rhine-*

stones, Gloves, Fabulous Hats, Feather Boas, Wigs, Makeup, Costumes, Fans, Purses, Cigarette Holders and More!

The sights of the city were complimented by the sounds of bebop on the local jazz station squeaking out of the car's tinny speakers—the vibrations of the brass, of the string-plucks of the upright bass and the *rat-a-tat-tat* of ghost notes spattering off the skin of the snare struggled to squeeze through the microscopic plastic holes of the car's speaker covers—

"Oop-pop-a-da…" scatted Dizzy Gillespie, in between the discordant squeals of the golden horns. San Francisco's Mid-Twentieth Century Renaissance had passed, but the sights and sounds hadn't really changed; its rhythm was the same.

It was this rhythm that the Beats chased—the Beats chased the rhythm and the rhythm chased the beats—the beats the Beats were after. They chased it from New York to San Francisco to Paris.

Jasper was chasing after the same thing; he was heading toward it, at least in name.

Those Beat writers, Kerouac, Burroughs, Ginsberg, and the other cats, their writing was jazz, it was free form—they were part of a movement, which implied a community or togetherness, but they were all doing their own thing, just like those jazz musicians on stage. It was spontaneous; *the first thought is the best thought*. Unpredictable, chaotic, but together it worked. The harmony of disharmony is often all the more harmonious—disharmony is life, it's bebop, it's the heartbeat. And that's what propelled Jasper, that's what he was after: life; specifically, a life that had been hidden from him, which he was only now rediscovering.

Beat up. Beat down. Perhaps, physically. But spiritually? It was all about beatitude. Beatific. Beatify. Beatification.

Dig? The core of the soul comes down to one thing: *the beat*. The beat is what keeps everything together.

While the Beats were intrigued by Eastern religion, perhaps the one unifying element of all faiths is the quest to find order, and subsequently establish that order, amidst the chaos of the world. If that's the standard, jazz most definitely qualifies as a religion. Jackson Pollack listened to it when he dripped, flicked and splattered a hodgepodge of paint onto an altar of canvas beneath him. Just as guaranteed as the bestowal of death and deadlines for taxes, the foundation of life is cemented in chaos. Nonetheless, people are biologically predisposed to project order onto the things around them, because order implies meaning, and meaning is what we seek. For a world without meaning—well, you know how that goes.

Blythe knocked on the door of 128 Clayton Street, Apartment 3F, behind which held that existential meaning for Jasper.

In this case, any morsel of meaning that might be derived was still just a projection, and Jasper was aware of that fact—it was still a pre-butterfly caterpillar. But it was human nature to hope its metamorphosis into the butterfly would happen sooner rather than later.

It was also human nature to digest itself inside its own metaphorical chrysalis before such a miracle could occur.

There was a slowing of time within Jasper's mind—to Jasper, Blythe's knocks were more in sync to the hourly chimes of Notre Dame or some such gothic institution with a modicum of cultural weight. He craned his head, absorbing the architecture, waiting for the door's locks to spin, while also hoping no one would be there to spin them; again, human nature.

Jasper stared at the floor. He stared at the squares and rectangles in the floor, light greens with iridescent gold highlights, layered under a cracked patina of grime—everything about it aching to be Art Deco.

The floor he was looking at in this hallway, inside this apartment building, was linoleum, or a faux-linoleum, because these days even cheap linoleum had been replaced by even cheaper, chemically derived materials. Real linoleum was made of organic materials—flammable, but organic materials—like the resin from pine trees, cork dust and wood flour, all in an effort to create a product of interior design that looked perfectly fake.

Just as the floors hinted at the luster of the floors of the 50's and 60's, Jasper's brain pined for what was, but not for what he remembered what was. He pined for what he did not remember. If he were ever to remember what was—and he knew there was a chance that part of his life, his real life, would be lost forever—he knew he had to confront what was behind this door.

That human nature thing? Procrastination is a big part of it, bigger than any of us realize. It was a whole hell of a lot easier for Jasper to lose himself in the patterns beneath his feet than to confront the pattern inside of him, the pattern that before long might manifest itself in front of his eyes, in the form of his daughter.

Much to Jasper's relief, a scraggly, bespectacled slacker, who most definitely was not Paris, opened the door.

"Aloha," muttered the slacker.

Jasper, taking in a quick breath, summoned his charisma, "Hey, man. We're looking for Paris, she around?"

"Nope."

Jasper inched his way inside the apartment, scanning the interior: kitchen, dining room, living room, all interconnected. The place was small. "Do you know when she'll be back?" He asked, spotting two decorative wooden masks on the wall—one smiling, one frowning, the Greek Muses of comedy and tragedy.

"Who are you guys?" the slacker asked, in such a way as to imply, *I didn't invite you in; however, I'm too much of a pussy to ask you to leave.*

"We're agents..." Jasper glanced over at the kitchen counter, which was home to a cluttered stack of eight-by-ten glossies: headshots of Paris. "...talent agents." He extended his hand to the slacker, which the discombobulated hipster shook eagerly—the kid's attitude turned on a dime.

"I'm Jonathan Fitch, and this is my associate, Claire Hutchinson. We're from FHA."

"For real?" the slacker asked.

"Real."

"Right. On." He pumped his head vigorously. "So, you guys make house calls? It's a bit unusual, don'tch'ya think?"

"The entertainment business isn't like other businesses," Blythe added. "There really aren't any rules."

"I can dig that." This seemed to make perfect sense to him. "Man, I wish Paris was around, I'm sure she'd wanna meet you. Shit. But she's gone for the night."

"You know where we can find her?"

"She's performing tonight—performing at her day job; well, night job, I guess is what you'd call it."

"Where?"

***

The Rotten Orange: fading neon letters framed within flashing orange bulbs illuminated the sign of this dive in Lower Haight. On the outside, it was San Francisco's equivalent to Las Vegas' Circus Circus—Dr. Hunter S. Thompson's screwball version of it—but on the inside, this joint substituted gambling for go-go-dancers. Jasper and

Blythe weaved through the spirited crowd inside, which was an eclectic, but unique, mix of bikers and hipsters. Vegetable-tanned leather, soda-bottle glasses, straw fedoras and endless swaths of tattooed skin peppered the room.

The decor was part carnival, part titty-bar, and the balance was surprisingly agreeable.

Jasper and Blythe perched themselves at a table near an elevated stage outfitted with a single stripper pole and mirrors galore, a number of which were broken. On the stage, a robust man with a Salvador Dali mustache and crimson bowtie snapped a bullwhip at a scantily clad woman with balloons taped over the expanse of her body. He cracked the whip, busting the last of the few remaining balloons with pinpoint precision. The limp remnants of deflated rubber covered her most intimate of parts as she squatted down and retrieved the pieces that got away from her.

The ringleader and surrealist doppelganger took her hand, helping her to stand up; they both took an unhurried bow. A large sign lit up above them: "We Appreciate Your Tips." The patrons applauded, rather modestly for such an enthralling act, and commenced the ritualistic tossing of crumpled up one-dollar bills onto the stage.

Chauncy Childress, a blind Lou Adler, white beard, black wrap-around glasses, and seeing eye German Shepherd, walked out on stage with a microphone in hand—

"Thank you ladies and gentlemen..."

The applause halted as Jasper and Blythe observed with a shared curiosity that just stopped short of peculiar.

"Please welcome the seductress of the shadows, the thrilla' in vanilla, the negro of the night, the harlot of the orient, the ass-kicka' from Aff-rikka, the buzzsaw from Arkansas, the samurai of Dubai, the shinobi of Nairobi..." He hushed his tone, in the service of drama, but didn't hush it much, "...her skills perfected in the hidden moun-

tains of the East. The dangerous, the invisible... the everyone."

As he paused, Jasper leaned forward in expectation. Chauncy took a great deal of pleasure in his pauses, that much was clear. It wasn't Shakespearean, but his routine proved more than adequate for the venue. He continued his monologue, with gravitas in his voice—

"Koga Ryu..."

Chauncy stumbled off the side of the stage as the over-head lights dimmed, focusing the audience's pupils for the upcoming performance. Sonic Youth's noise-rock anthem, *100%*, began to blast through the house speakers. Thurston Moore's discordant Fender Jazzmaster guitar buzzed and screeched. Then the figure of a woman strutted onto the stage. She was lit from behind, her slender frame in sil-houette; she moved and manipulated her body as though she, herself, was the manifestation of Moore's distorted notes.

This girl *was* sonic youth.

Sound waves were her blood cells, and this transfusion of grunge roused the rhythm in her limbs, her hips, her head, her entire fucking body. She spun across the back wall, almost sticking to it via static electricity or some freak redirection of gravity, waving her arms behind her back and over her head, and pumping her legs as the drums and lyrics kicked in, "*I can never forget you...*"

The audience looked on, visibly on edge; for Jasper, the jury was still out, but his interest was no less piqued.

"*...the way you rock the girls.*"

In the midst of the shadows, the woman catapulted to the top of the pole, hooking her legs onto it. She hung there, upside-down, exhibiting an admirable amount of calf strength as she pressed her legs against the cold metal—

Until she monkey-dropped, headfirst toward the floor.

A monkey drop, at first, looks like an accident, a slip in a stripper's grip that leads to an exhilarating and seemingly careless freefall, but when executed well, it's a magnificent jolt. Just before her head could introduce itself to the floor, she flipped herself over into a perfect sitting position, facing the audience.

A spotlight crackled to life, its circle striking the woman and illuminating her face to the patrons around her: it was Paris.

There was a brightness to her, and not as a result of the light—the short jet-black hair with blue streaks of blue that framed her round cheekbones and cloaked her sinuous neck suggested an innocence that was once there, but was now long gone.

"Can you forgive the boy who… shot you in the head?"

She pursed her lips at the crowd, and then slammed the heels of her black pumps together like Dorothy in *The Wizard of Oz*, only much, much dirtier.

"Or should you get a gun and… go and get revenge?"

Jasper was taken aback; Blythe shifted awkwardly in her chair, uncrossing and recrossing her legs. Paris sprung to her feet and pivoted around, introducing the audience to all three-hundred-and-sixty degrees of her.

"One hundred percent of my love."

Barely a day over eighteen, she was clearly athletic—as evidenced by her knack for acrobatics—but she also had just the right amount of curve. Rocking sleeves of tattoos and a frilly get-up that was both Marilyn Monroe and Manson, she spun herself around the pole before slamming her back against the buckling ground. Writhing like a rattlesnake, she brought a knee into the center of her chest. She worked her knee back and forth between her bosom; it looked like it hurt, and it was unclear whether this was supposed to turn on or turn off the audience.

Running her hands along her fishnets and the camouflage leg warmers she wore over them, Paris pulled a long,
thin object from her garter. She sat straight up and stashed
the item in her mouth, gripping it tightly between her teeth.
Bending forward, she began to crawl like a tomcat toward
several titillated fellows waving legal tender at the foot of
the stage.

*"But I've been around the world a million times, and all you men
are slime. It's the gun to my head, goodbye I am dead, Wastewood
rockers is time for cryin'... "*

She sat down, bringing her knees together—
"Hey!"

As the drum breakdown kicked in, the place went completely strobe. Jasper recoiled, instinctually bringing a hand
to his face, attempting to shield his eyes from the flashing
light. His focus was immediately lost; any attempt to retain
it was out of his control. It was like he was only seeing
fragments of the visual information that was unfolding
around him.

Paris removed the item from her mouth. Jasper squinted
through the gaps in his fingers, as he continued to look in
her direction, but the action around him nevertheless trick-
led into his retinas. In one swift motion, Paris snapped her
wrist at the ground as she spread her legs apart: between
them was an oriental fan that she had opened.

Jasper snapped his attention to the fan, his mind sweeping him from this time and place—

Instantaneously, he was bombarded with a series of stac-
cato images that were in sync with the strobe: a little girl,
who looked about the age of five, in a sun-drenched backyard, casually dressed in overalls and pigtails. These images
materialized in the middle of Jasper's mind's eye, and the
point of view was distinct. The point of view, as though it

was being seen through the eyes of another, playfully chased the girl around a weeping willow tree.

The perspective was Jasper's—*it had to be*—and the little girl was Paris—*it had to be.*

Jasper couldn't be wholly sure, objectively speaking, if this girl was Paris, his flesh and blood, but it wasn't an objective question; Jasper knew simply because he knew. He could feel it. As this little girl, Paris, hopped onto a swing suspended from the tree, he could just feel it.

As Jasper closed in on little Paris, she whipped open an oriental fan, one that was not dissimilar to the fan her older self opened just moments ago in the club. She attempted to hide herself beneath its folds. She peeked over the top of the fan, smiling up at her father—

Jasper, blinking his eyes against the light, snapped out of his stupor as the strobes inside The Rotten Orange came to a stop. The men ogling Paris showered her with crumpled cash. Jasper was breathing rapidly; he was having a hard time catching his breath.

Paris gripped the pole and propelled herself upward. Her momentum spun her around as she arched her back to the pole, corkscrewing down it elegantly like the red stripe of a candy cane. She landed, her back to the audience. She fanned herself in profile as everyone in the room cheered her on.

Jasper did not cheer. He was focused on the area at the small of her back—he was focused on her Japanese tattoo.

***

Moments later, in an alcove adjacent to the performers' dressing rooms, Blythe waited for Jasper. He gradually stepped toward her. "Can you give me some time…with her?" he asked.

"You have a few hours."

Jasper nodded, grateful, but still hesitant; Blythe gave the damp palm of his hand a squeeze. "Call me on a hard line," she said.

As Jasper released her hand, she brushed her arm against his side; he was oblivious as to whether the move was accidental or an aborted attempt at a hug. Either way it was sliced, Jasper liked the feeling of being close to another human being at this moment. Perhaps he was projecting, perhaps he was hoping to achieve the same feeling with Paris, a regaining of a connection, of an unpliable bond, or perhaps it was a reaction that had been implanted in him, a reaction that couldn't be trusted on a physiological level, a reaction that reinforced the belief in something that never was, nor ever would be. But Jasper knew it was the belief in the opposite, in something that was and would be, whether genuine or fake, that encourages people to ignore such facts, and as a result, achieve some sort of happiness in life.

Ignorance is bliss—or so the ignorant say.

Jasper gradually weaved his way through a gaggle of showgirls and into a cramped room at the end of a constricted hallway. Blythe watched him go, before walking out of the place.

Paris was stoic as she sat in front of a cracked illumination mirror—*it's only bad luck if you cracked it*—gathering her personal items, which consisted mostly of an assortment of neon lip glosses and eyeliner pencils. Jasper gradually approached her from behind, "Paris?"

Paris looked up, meeting eyes with Jasper, connected through the glass of the mirror. "Yes?" she said, matter-of-factly.

"Paris Robertson?"

"The name is Childress. Paris Childress." She waited a moment, presumably awaiting a response from this inquiring man. There have been many—too many—inquiring men in the past, especially in the hallowed halls of this hole. "If you're not gonna tell me who you are and what you want, you can get the hell out of my dressing room."

Jasper stepped a few inches closer, leaning over her slightly, "Are you the daughter of Cynthia Robertson?"

Paris splintered at the mention of the name. She grabbed the oriental fan from on top of her makeup kit and faced Jasper.

In an instant, her arms were in the air, throwing a combination of punches at tonight's target. Jasper reacted just as instantly, blocking each one of them as he shuffled backwards. She kept coming at him, pushing him further and further back.

As he obstructed another strike, she kicked the inside of his left ankle, setting him off balance and causing him to stumble. The backs of his shoulders slammed into the wall.

Paris snapped open her fan and quickly brought the outer edge of it toward his neck. Jasper slapped his hands together, as if in prayer, and wedged them between his neck and the fan, blocking the fashion accessory. They looked into each other's eyes in a stalemate.

Paris continued to push the fan toward him, the silk compressing around his hands as concealed iron spikes began to protrude from the fan ribs. Two of the spikes extended around his hands toward the bottoms of his eyes, their barbed tips stopping within an inch of his pupils.

Jasper was calm; his demeanor might have seemed unusual to some, but it wasn't to him. He was cool and collected, almost smiling; it was as if he were testing her.

"Where did you learn how to do that?" he asked.

Paris looked at him, a tear dripping from her eye: "My father taught me."

Jasper thought he knew before; now he knew for sure. Paris had known who he was the second she saw him.

93

CHAPTER SEVEN

INSIDE OF Paris's apartment, her slacker roommate lounged on the couch, his gorilla-like legs slung up on an ottoman, popping popcorn into his mouth. He watched the *breaking news* on the centerpiece of their living room, a sixty-two inch flat screen television with a shitty set of surround sound speakers—

"The unsettling revelation of President Rafferty's mental illness has sent shockwaves throughout Washington," the anchor, a zaftig woman in a polyester pantsuit, explained to the camera as a window next to her image recycled a clip of a press conference. "White House Press Secretary, Glenn Stephenson, was quick to address what was leaked to the media earlier this afternoon."

Glenn Stephenson addressed a room of restless reporters in the White House briefing room—

"The President has dealt with acute social anxiety disorder for most of her adult life. Just this past year, she joined millions of other Americans in being diagnosed with clinical depression. In light of the recent leak to the media, President Rafferty wanted me to strongly convey that this diagnosis has no bearing whatsoever on her ability to run the government and lead this nation. In fact, with the aid of medication prescribed by her personal physician, she has never been more focused and in command. I can assure you—we can all assure you—that she is as strong as ever."

Paris walked into her apartment, Jasper in tow.

The slacker dude craned his head toward them. "Hey Par." The way he craned his neck, it was like his head weighed two tons; it seemed to have taken quite a bit of effort, and was likely a result of the liberal portion of purple haze he smoked earlier in the evening. He dropped his glasses to the tip of his nose, peering over them at Jasper: "Fuckin' A. You got yourself some representation, huh? Does this mean I can't call you anymore—gotta go through your agent now? That shit's fucking bomb."

Paris laughed, chuckling away his idiocy, a vocalization that often preceded her "hello" when it came to this dude. "Hey, Blake, are you heading out?"

Okay, the slacker's name was Blake, Jasper thought to himself. Not that he particularly gave a shit, though the name did seem an appropriate match to the character depicted before him.

"Nah," Blake responded.

"You mind giving us a few minutes? We kinda have to talk business."

"I get it." He rapped on the side of his head with his knuckles. "I'll get out of your hair." He stood up and popped a clove cigarette with a gold-wrapped filter into his mouth. "I was just watching some weird shit about the President—turns out she's some kind of loon."

"That is weird."

"What's weirder is that's considered 'breaking news'— fucking interrupted the Manchester United game."

Blake grabbed a tattered leather jacket, whipped it over his shoulder and headed out of the apartment. "Hasta." As he opened the door, he turned to Jasper, "Don't be taking more than ten percent…or that's some bogus horse-puck." He shut the door behind him, as if for emphasis, or for whatever.

Paris veered into the kitchen. Looking at Jasper, she gestured a hand toward the sunken couch. Jasper obliged her form of sign language and took a seat. He picked up where Blake left off, consuming the breaking news on the roommates' most prized possession—

The anchorwoman conversed with the network's resident medical correspondent, Dr. Nils Mikkels, a stiff with a slumber-inducing voice: "Does this call into question her ability to lead?"

"In the disclosure statement that was issued to the media," Dr. Mikkels responded, "it indicates that the President has been prescribed 'Tymatrope,' the wildly popular, and I might add, wildly successful, anti-anxiety medication for just over the past year."

Jasper cocked his head at the mention of "Tymatrope," the lids of his eyes fluttering a bit, involuntarily.

The news report cut to an on-the-street interview with a supporter of the President, a young mother leaning on a baby carriage—her face was as puerile and unembellished as her baby's. She leaned into the microphone: "It just makes me like her even more. She's a human being. People forget that. I've known friends and family members who were depressed, and medication saved their lives."

"You want something to drink?" Paris asked.

"Whatever you're having." Jasper was engrossed by the television, staring at it, listening to it, absorbing it.

"With advancements in pharmaceuticals like antidepressants, these days mental illness or whatever you wanna call it, it's a thing of the past."

Paris placed a glistening bottle of Negra Modelo—Mexico's Guinness and a favorite of Bay Area bohemians—on the coffee table in front of Jasper, which rerouted his attention to Paris. His eyes traced her arm, scanning the intricately drawn lines of a medusa tattoo, the turquoise snakes sprouting from its head leading his eyes to his daughter's shoulder, across her collarbone, up her neck and into the alcoves of her eyes. He could not help but stare at her.

"You changed your name?"

"It's Chauncy's last name." She plopped down on the recliner across from him. "He's taken good care of me."

"The guy who runs that place? I can see that he cares about your go-go dancing career."

"No, that was my idea," Paris said, smirking. "He wants me to go to law school." She stared back at Jasper, into his own alcoves, recesses that sheltered eyes as lifeless as a reptile's; from her perspective, at any rate. "I thought you were dead."

"I was dead."

She just looked at him; she was used to men lying to her, and her expression was one that had become stock. She pulled it off the shelves when she needed to, which was more often than she would like.

"I mean, whoever I was before is dead. It's like my life's been erased—you probably know a lot more about me than I do." He tried to plead with whatever life could be mustered in his eyes: "What's my name?"

"Are you serious?" She burst into a fit of laughter: "You're fucking with me."

She sipped her beer as he just continued to stare at her; this kind of morbidly sentimental staring was getting old quick.

"Sam. Sam Robertson," she said.

"I guess that's better than Jasper."

"Your name is Jasper?"

Jasper shrugged his shoulders.

"Named after a rock," she said; her tone may very well have been sarcastic, but it was impossible for Jasper to tell.

"Appropriate," he responded.

"Which fascist government agency did this to you? CIA? FBI? Al Qaeda?" Paris snickered to herself, shaking her head back and forth. "You told me you were a stuntman, which is why you were away all the time."

Jasper could only sit there and listen; there was nothing for him to recall, not on his own, in any case.

"We used to go to the movies when I was a kid and you'd point yourself out to me, in the big action scenes, when the real actor would be sitting on the sidelines, catching Z's in his trailer. But, of course, I'd never recognize you because those Hollywood producers go out of their way to disguise you, right? Make you look just like the actor, or shoot you from behind. I thought I recognized your back, or the side of your head, sometimes a hand. But I was wrong. It wasn't you."

Paris was getting choked up. Jasper wished he were.

"It was never you." she said.

"Sorry. I don't remember that."

"You don't even know what you're saying sorry for!"

Paris stood up, towering over him, both physically and emotionally.

"I need to know where your mother is? That's why I'm here."

"My mother? My mother is dead!"

Jasper stood up as well, trying to reason with her, struggling with the imagery that had been repeating over and over in his head. "No," he insisted.

"She committed suicide."

"You thought I was dead," he said, struggling with the information. "How did they tell you I died?"

"Get out," she whispered.

"Your mother might be alive. If she is, I need to find her—and I'm going to need your help."

She dropped her head into her chest, peering down to the floor.

"Only a day or two ago, I was a web designer with an overwhelming feeling that something was missing from my life. Something I could never quite figure out. Until now… Until I found you."

"Get out!" Paris shouted at him.

Jasper accommodated her request—he was expecting it, frankly—and walked out of the apartment without much hesitation. Paris crouched down, dropping to the floor and curling into a tight little ball. She began sobbing; the kind of sobbing that strangles the tears of the sobber.

***

The location: Fisherman's Wharf. Blythe sat pensively on a neglected city bench and gazed across the wharf, Alcatraz looming securely in the distance. A man approached her; she was confident that she, and only she, was aware of this person's identity amongst the pedestrians and hobos— hobos who would surely vie for her spot on the bench as soon as she left it. His visage was obscured in the darkness and his long camel hair coat seemed to swallow any hint of a persona.

Blythe casually twisted her body to face him. "We're running on schedule," she said to him.

The man removed his coat and placed it over Blythe's bare shoulders. She was trembling, ever so slightly, but her trembling was noticeable. The air that coasted off the water at the wharf could do that to a person. The man could only presume this to be the cause of Blythe's trembles; to think otherwise would be to weigh on the side of suspicion—and suspicion in this business was the beginning of the end of what could only be called trust.

***

Under the cover of what darkness was available in this Northern California metropolis, a procession of armored black vans pulled up to the curb opposite Paris's apartment complex. This had the effect of creating a vehicular wall obstructing the pedestrian view of the building from the sidewalk.

Inside the building, Jasper lurched down the interior hall outside of Paris's apartment door. He headed straight to the elevator, pressed the down button, and lingered there. He mulled over the time, however brief it was, that he had just spent with his daughter, his biological offspring. He was more attuned than ever to time and its fleeting temperament. While he remained unable to recall the memories he, presumably, had of his daughter when she was growing up, he ruminated on the possibility that this interaction with his daughter may be the only memory he had, or will ever have, of her.

This scared the shit out of him.

For a man who had apparently been trained not to be scared, this was a staggering insight. While his memories were still locked up wherever they were, his feelings were beginning to come back, and coming back in droves, surging through him like shots of adrenaline.

The elevator door opened like stage curtains, revealing Paris's roommate, Blake, splayed out on the floor, unconscious. Jasper hit a knee, placing a hand on his neck, grasping for a pulse.

He turned the young man's head from one side to the other. There was no question: he was dead.

The lights in the hallway ceiling began to flicker. Jasper squinted away from it; he wouldn't let his mind be lifted from him again like it was in the club. Not in this moment. This was the kind of moment he had been manufactured to confront and, summarily, neutralize. As disturbing as it was for him to acknowledge, this hypothesis brought him comfort.

The flickering stopped. The lights went out. Jasper opened his eyes.

He sprinted back up the dark hall to Paris's door. Without a second passing through his perception of time, he threw his foot up and jackhammered it through her door. The frame splintered, the circa 1970's deadbolt no match for even a tenth of his force.

Paris stood in the middle of the dim living room as Jasper rushed inside. "What in the hell is going on?" she demanded to know.

Jasper pressed a finger to the outside of his lips. "Fire escape?" he asked, in a whisper.

Paris set her emotions aside, quickly detecting there were other stakes at play. She pointed her finger toward a set of windows, a triptych of moonlight, across the living room. Jasper grabbed hold of her arm and pulled her over to them. He opened the far right window, and then swung her against the wall beside it, making sure she was out of sight. He drew his .9mm from the back of his pants.

"When I tell you to, I want you to get out that window and get down those ladders as quickly as possible. Do you understand?"

"I'm not gonna take orders from you."

"You better start."

Paris hesitated, sensing his seriousness. He waited for a moment, listening, and then, he nodded: "Go!"

She whipped her body around his and hurdled herself out the window and onto the fire escape. Jasper squatted down, peering outside, resting his arm on the sill and aiming his gun at the building across the street. As Paris shimmied down the ladders, like a squirrel scuttling down the bark of a tree, Jasper traced his aim from windowsill to windowsill, focusing in on a shadowy outline in an open window.

He fired—

He hit the outline, an outline that dropped from the window, a long-range rifle gripped in its hands.

Gunshots rang out across the street; it was a horizontal Fourth of July. Jasper dropped to the floor as a brick beside the window shattered, its jagged particles flying haphazardly into the living room. He calmly rose, standing directly in front of the window. He scanned the building again, spotting the spark of a muzzle flash from the adjacent roof. He homed in on it, reflexively firing—his little .9mm collapsing the sniper with a fatal headshot.

Tilting his body out the window, Jasper peered down at Paris. She cleared the final rung of the last ladder and hopped onto the pavement.

Jasper stuck his gun back in his pants and hastened after her. He didn't so much step as fly down the fire escape— bypassing the entire point of the ladders themselves—dropping from one platform to another in rapid succession. Bullets peppered the bricks framed around him. He evaded the shots, enlisting gravity as his accomplice, Sir Isaac Newton, his getaway driver. When he hit the ground, he turned and spotted Paris crouched anxiously behind a nearby sedan.

"Let's go," Jasper said.

They booked down the sidewalk. Jasper pulled his gun, extending his arm as he ran, aiming his weapon's barrel at the other side of the street. There was some *almost* imperceptible movement in an alleyway across from them. Jasper fired three shots, seemingly at nothing, to Paris's eyes. Two men in ski masks stumbled from the mouth of the alley, falling to the garbage-strewn ground, blood seeping out of them and into the cracks of the sidewalk.

Paris, stunned, glanced back at Jasper as they continued to run.

They turned the nearest corner and scoped an oncoming cable car, a bygone specimen of San Francisco's Municipal Railway, as it chugged along its northbound route. Jasper hopped onto the red, white and gold tourist trap, bringing Paris with him, as it crept its way up the steep hill.

"You can't just jump up here like that, it's dangerous..." the skinny black gripman protested, shouting over the scratchy recording of *I Left My Heart In San Francisco* that reverberated through speakers hanging from the corners of the car. "*High on a hill, it calls to me/To be where little cable cars climb halfway to the stars!*"

The tune was likely set on an endless loop; a loop Jasper was about to bring to a resounding end. "*The morning fog may chill the air/I don't care!*"

Jasper whipped out his gun, pointing it at the wooden ceiling. "Everybody get down!"

The conductor materialized from the opposite end of the car, an older black gentleman with the requisite hat, holding his quivering hands in the air, "Everyone do what he says…we don't want any…trouble."

The gripman and a handful of passengers hit the deck, some of them screaming, or trying to scream, as the tips of bullets fired by someone other than Jasper began popping against the sides of the car. The pops were earsplitting.

Jasper ran to the front of the car and waved his gun near the side of the conductor's head.

"On the floor."

The humpbacked man dropped to the floor as the car maintained its slow but steady course uphill. Two black vans approached from behind, preparing to simultaneously flank the cable car. Jasper, taking a millisecond to think, kicked out a window and yanked the billboard off the outside of the car. He pulled the hefty advertisement for athletic foot cream, which featured a rather unphotogenic set of toes beset with fungus, inside the car with relative ease.

The gripman sat up slightly, his fingers weaved behind his head, "I gotta drop the cable before the next inter-section, or I'm gonna cut the other line."

"What does that mean?" Jasper responded.

"I gotta let go of the grip."

Jasper didn't have time for this shit.

"It means it'll cut through the street's cable, fuck the whole line up—jeopardize the other cars, fuckin' shit-storm."

"If you haven't noticed, the shitstorm's already started, and it's happening right here." Jasper said, bluntly.

The lead van was heading south on the street. Agent Ito was riding in its passenger seat, in the colloquial *shotgun*. The vehicle was driving uphill, heading toward the hijacked cable car, which was out of sight on the other side of the hill.

The entire city was wired—it was *big-city-electric*. Under-neath its streets ran an entirely subterranean ecosystem of multi-directional horsepower. The concrete buzzed with life, albeit a consistent 9.5 miles per hour of life, but at least it was consistent, and in that sense, immortal. Immortal lest its power station proved fallible. In essence, the power was the cable's deity, and in the context of this city, the omni-present god of San Francisco. The conductor and gripman were the high priests of this travelling altar; the city's tourists, its congregation, bowing down in worship to the wire rope.

The cable cars merely gripped onto the wires under-ground and surrendered themselves to their respective des-tinations via a system of pulleys and sheaves through which the wires weaved their ways throughout the municipality.

The cable car was travelling toward a problem. The ap-proaching cross street's wire ran over their line, requiring the gripman to *drop* the rope and *jump* the line and *re-grip* it once it was cleared, otherwise their car would slice through the cable. On top of that, the car had to jump at just the right moment, once it crested the hill, or it risked losing its momentum and coasting backwards, and if the conductor and gripman were not in control of the brakes, that would be bad news.

As the car approached the summit of the hill, Ito's ve-hicle approached the same summit, on the opposite side, poised for a potential collision. Ito had one hand on the grip of the door and the other on a pair of large night-vision goggles that were strapped to his face. Through these goggles, he observed the cable car as it finally came into view—he focused on a bright, greenish image that he was able to magnify, zooming into Jasper and Paris as the agency's other vans sandwiched the trolley.

As he closed in on their enhanced images, Jasper and Paris dropped like a couple of flesh bricks to the floor.

Ito, leaning on the edge of his seat, examined the cable car through his relatively limited view. It was as though, suddenly, no one was on board.

On the floor of the cable car, the gripman reached his arm up toward the grip lever. Just as the car plateaued, he pulled it back, dropping the rope. He breathed a slight sigh of relief.

Ito's vehicle moved closer and closer, about to converge on the cable car. "Damn-it," Ito mumbled, bracing for impact as his driver cut the van's wheel.

At the tail's end of the cable car, Jasper peeled himself from the floor and heaved the billboard over the rear banister, holding onto the end of it as it dragged against the coarse pavement. As he centered it over the street, Paris leaped over the ornate banister and landed the soles of her feet on the billboard.

Jasper glanced back over his shoulder, watching the lead van skid, its tires screeching, sliding sideways toward the trolley. Inertia had taken control of the federal vehicle, amongst other things.

Seconds before the van was to collide with the cable car, Jasper released his grip on the advertisement, sliding Paris along the street atop the cardboard. She rode the advertisement as though she were surfing—or some post-apocalyptic version of the watersport sans the water—but the pavement underneath was just rigid enough to knock her to one knee.

When she was far enough away, Jasper grabbed a commuter pole, holding onto it and the cable car it was connected to, as the lead van rammed into the front of the car. Everyone on the floor of the cable car slid toward the front like plastic dolls in an antique wooden box that had just tumbled from an attic shelf. The car's vice-like grip underneath the street had been disabled—with the men in charge having been hurled across their vessel, the car acquiesced to the centrifugal force inflicted upon it by Ito's van. It practically lifted from the tracks as it was rocket-shot back to where it came from: down the upside of street.

Jasper gripped the pole in much the same way as the cable car gripped the wire below, with routine assurance and a level of certainty that it, unfortunately, didn't have at this specific moment.

Inside one of the flanking vans, the driver glanced into his side-view mirror and spotted Paris scraping down the street. "She's on the street!" he shouted into his headset. The agent to his immediate right cocked his machine gun and unfastened his torso from his seatbelt.

Jasper only had a fraction of a second to act; but for his new self, it felt more like a few minutes, or a second or two that had been stretched out via a slow-motion application implanted in his brain. He calculated, then carried out the calculation.

As the cable car freewheeled down the street, its useless underbelly mechanics dragging and sparking along the blacktop, Jasper hopped its rear banister and leapt onto the back bumper of the right flanking van as it passed. The vehicle curved away from the cable car, heading back down the street. All eyes were on Paris and the cable car that was skating toward her. Jasper used the rear windshield wiper to balance himself as he opened the trunk and hurdled into the back of the van.

Jasper dove down as the agent in the front passenger seat swung backwards and unloaded the entire clip of his gun into the trunk.

"He's in the back of the car!"

The driver maintained his cool, continuing to head toward Paris as he tried to outrun the rogue cable car.

Jasper crawled toward the agent taking aim at him, popping up a few degrees left of his weapon and discharging a bullet of his own through the agent's neck.

As the driver twisted around, or tried to, struggling to orient himself to the vehicle's intruder, Jasper slammed the butt of his weapon into the bulge of skull behind the man's right ear. The sickening crack of his bone accompanied the man's instantaneous collapse into the dashboard.

On the street, Paris peered over her shoulder at the cable car on her ass. She skidded to a stop and sprang up from the board. As she dashed across a mostly deserted intersecting avenue, the cable car came soaring past her, leveling her makeshift surfboard—or *streetboard*, if she were tasked to brand the apparatus.

Inside the cable car, the conductor was out cold; the gripman, however, got a second wind—it was a second wind that might have been his last if he didn't get up and pull the brakes. He crawled to the emergency brake and tugged it, jamming up the street slot and stopping the car.

He looked up, noticing another cable car within a few feet of his own, its cluster of tourist passengers standing with mouths agape.

As Paris booked down the adjacent street, she looked behind her: a black van, its headlights glaring, had her in its sights. She ran like hell, but the van was next to her almost immediately. She was nearly out of breath.

She glanced over to it as it came to rest beside her—she couldn't help it; it was self-preservation, not curiosity—as the passenger door swung open.

"Get in!"

She peered up at Jasper behind the driver's wheel of the van. She didn't think twice; she jumped into the vehicle, not wasting any time, and shut the door closed behind her.

The sounds of police sirens rose into the ether as the left flanking van made a last ditch effort to turn itself around. It haphazardly swerved into a swath of oncoming traffic, opening itself up to a speeding police cruiser arriving on the scene. The cruiser sideswiped the van, spinning it right back around.

This was about the time that first responders and an excess of agency backup began to surround the area. In what seemed like a matter of moments, the place was a mob scene. Jasper turned his van down an alley, as inconspicuously as he could, and disappeared into the night.

Rendered inert at the summit of the hill, the door of the lead van creaked open and Ito stepped out, his legs casting the impression he was standing atop shaky ground, the muscles in his limbs quivering. It became clear that his spasming was not the result of trauma, but rather the product of inexplicable rage—rage at the handling of this entire situation. The wire ropes beneath his skin moved faster than San Francisco's 9.5 miles an hour and he was struggling to maintain his grip on them. He was beginning to lose control of something he had been in complete control of for what might as well be the measurement of Jasper's existence.

Ripping the goggles from his head, he threw them to the ground in abject frustration. He stared down the concrete hill: Jasper and Paris were nowhere in sight, and wouldn't be for quite a while, he gathered.

Jasper drove through the streets of this uneven city, evading the force that sought his capture, as Paris slumped in the passenger seat. Her nerve endings were caught inside an epidermal cyclone. Her skin felt like someone else's, and she felt sorry for that someone else, that poor bitch, because getting her shit together may, in fact, be impossible.

Physically, and mentally, she was wiped. She rolled down her window and attempted a breath, extracting as much oxygen from the air that her lungs could manage, and leaned her throbbing head onto Jasper's shoulder.

Jasper pretended not to notice, but of course, that was all he noticed.

CHAPTER EIGHT

PARIS LED Jasper past the closed up front of The Rotten Orange, a security gate stretched across its dilapidated façade, to a side entrance of the building. They slid through a half-opened gate and descended a small set of cobblestone steps. There was a light fixture above their heads, but it sure as hell wasn't on. Paris squinted in the darkness and banged on the rusted door with her fist until the occupant on the other side was compelled to respond—

"Who is it? And why are you here so goddamn late?"

"I thought you never sleep, Chauncy," Paris replied.

"Metaphor." Chauncy said, as he slowly opened the door. "Hello, Paris."

Paris and Jasper shuffled into his bedraggled abode, a small apartment adjacent to the club. Chauncy turned in the direction of Jasper as he wrapped a black velvet robe around himself, tying a paisley belt at the waist. "Who is it I smell next to you?"

"This is Jasper." Paris said.

"Jasper. The rock. I was just sleeping like a rock. I was enjoying my third erection of the sleep cycle."

"Sorry to disturb you." Jasper said, not really all that apologetic.

"Chauncy, I need your help." Paris spoke in a voice as taut as her muscles, a tone she reserved for only the most serious of matters. Chauncy could not help but pick up on it.

"What kind of help?"

She hesitated for a moment, as if her response was somehow inevitable, before she went ahead and answered him: "The room."

Chauncy was immediately suspicious. Most late night visits, especially in Chauncy's part of town, gave rise to similar levels of dubiousness. Be that as it may, the man complied.

Chauncy opened the door to a sizeable walk-in closet, one he thought might make Imelda Marcos proud. He shoved aside a rack of extravagant costumes, boas and such, along with a translucent case of what appeared to be fake mustaches of varying sizes and styles. Jasper, considering his secret life as a spy, smiled at the mustaches. Had one of these spy novel clichés adorned his upper lip in the past? If so, how severe was it? Had he worn a handlebar mustache, and when he opted—*or was forced*—to wear such disguises, how much say did he have in the style?

His smile quickly disappeared when Chauncy revealed the small door built into the wall of the closet. It was now Jasper's turn to be suspicious. But before he could say or do anything, Paris brushed right past him, crouched down and opened the door.

"Come on."

She stepped through it, rather casually, followed by Chauncy; his attempt was casual, but when you're that old and physically compromised, moving around both looks and feels a lot harder than it used to be.

Jasper, the rock, didn't move much himself—he bent down, trying to get a decent look through the door.

"You heard the lady," Chauncy mumbled.

Jasper did as he was told. He hunched through the miniature hallway—the space was a glorified ventilation duct—and climbed down a ladder into a dank, dark, dead space. The sound was dead; there was virtually no reverberation. Chauncy flipped a light switch that illuminated a succession of fluorescent rods in the ceiling of this acoustically-challenged room.

Jasper blinked, as per his usual reaction to the unanticipated powering on of incandescence, and then took a look around—

It was a deep room that, at the present moment, was host to a stockpile of what had the appearance of martial arts weapons. It seemed as though the room was built specifically for these arms to line its walls. Weapons made of metal, weapons made of wood, weapons made of all kinds of materials, in threatening sizes and unequivocally dangerous shapes.

"What kind of trouble are you in?" Chauncy asked Paris, point-blank.

"This is my father."

Paris gestured to Jasper. Chauncy glanced at him—or, more accurately, glanced toward him—clearly taken aback. It even took Chauncy a second or two to remember his name: "Sam?"

"You know me?" Jasper responded.

"No. Not personally." Chauncy recycled through the memories residing in his relatively thick cranium, looking for bookmarks. "But the person who asked me to take Paris did."

"Who is that?"

Things were beginning to sink in for Jasper, the potholes in his brain were beginning to be filled; his sleep was wearing off. Chauncy was careful to respond, but responded nonetheless.

"Hiroshi Ito."

Jasper began to strain his brain for information, a road map to this name, but it was a useless endeavor.

"He trained me in the agency." Chauncy said.

"I don't know him," Jasper said.

"I do. He couldn't save my eyesight, but he did save my life. I was in demolitions."

Chauncy took a second to snicker; Jasper didn't snicker, but he wasn't entirely convinced either.

"No shit, right?" Chauncy continued. "I was part of an aborted op. Wiring and heating up a compromised safe house. Protocol was to leave me to die. Ito never much cared for protocol. I've been retired since. But you know what they say, you never really retire in this business." He took a moment to breathe, breathe without talking, which was something of a challenge for Chauncy. "I thought you were dead."

Paris, looking over at her father—

"So did I."

Jasper caught sight of a bronze-handled staff mounted on the wall: it was almost identical to his own staff. He approached the weapon, lifting it up.

"That is the shikomi chigirigi," Paris said.

Jasper rubbed the handle, a spherical grip similar in shape to his handle, on which boasted the same Japanese phrase.

"You trained me on that," Paris said. "It was always your favorite."

"It was, huh?"

"Well, you also told me martial arts was just a hobby."

Jasper looked at his daughter, and then began tracing the writing with his fingertip, "What is this…"

"The Koga Ryu," Paris said.

"Your stage name."

Paris nodded; there was a little bit of pride in her gesticulation, if you were in the room, you could tell.

Chauncy squatted down on the ground, gathering together his thoughts, thoughts that were most of the time loose, but in this moment tightened like a hangman's rope. "The Koga Ryu," Chauncy said, "assassins in the mountains of feudal Japan—masters of activities dishonorable enough that Japanese warriors hired others to perform them. The Koga Ryu were the others."

He paused; the old man and the dramatic pause were chums, the patrons of The Rotten Orange could attest to that. "They were like the Special Forces of the East; the Green Berets or Navy SEALs over here, before we conceived of such groups. Their last documented activity, as far as I'm aware, was in World War Two." He scratched himself vigorously behind the ears. "In the sixties, a small group of Koga reemerged, living in the Canadian Rockies before migrating down into the States. They blended in as businessmen, and other professional types, passing their secrets along to the few who were chosen."

"And before you left," Paris turned to Jasper, "you passed them down to me…"

Jasper had a hard time—a really fucking hard time—believing he was this expertly trained.

"I never knew why you were trained, or why you trained me. You never told me much."

"I never told her anything beyond what I thought she needed to know," Chauncy added.

Paris glanced at Chauncy. She couldn't hold this against him; her father was back, and the consequences of him being back had nearly gotten her killed. She had to deal with what was pressing, and that was staying alive.

She looked up at Jasper and called him: "Shidoshi."

Shidoshi means mentor, the closest aphorism to the word *father* that she knew, and would probably ever know.

Jasper gripped the shikomi chigirigi in his hands and thrust the handle outward. He watched it swing, dangling from its chain. The evidence was damning.

***

Koga Ryu, an ancient school of Ninjutsu. *Ninjutsu.* The root from which the term *Ninja* is derived.

Get over it.

It's a word, a description of someone you definitely do not want to run into. Not the Chuck Norris of the 80's, nor the Jackie Chan of the 90's, not even *the* Bruce Lee, who never purported to be a ninja in his films; he was a master of Wing Chun, an advanced mode of Kung Fu. The modern image of the ninja conjures a likeness more aligned with Halloween costumes—not to mention endless amounts of internet memes—it's the butt of jokes, not a source of intimidation, at least these days.

Jasper's mind had been wandering of late. Thoughts, superficially disparate, digressions, flowed randomly around his neural pathways, both between and intersecting each other, but finally connecting, in concrete fashion. Some thoughts he wrote down in his notebook, some he did not. Jasper had dreamed of France, or what he thought were French bodies of land. At first, his dreamscape was as foreign, and about as unrecognizable, as Japan—though one might find Japan to be pretty unique; it is about as alien a culture outside of America that any conjurer of lands, curator of cultures or maker of maps can create.

115

To confuse any section of Europe with it seemed unlike-
ly, yet Jasper could not be sure. No amount of neon lights
and rice-paper doors could tip the scales of his neurological
sense receptors. The conflation of these two cultures in his
mind, in his memory, seemed not only normal, but also
encouraged at a basic level.

But encouraged by whom? Or by what?

These questions led to assumptions, and these assumptions led to grandiose thoughts, which he doubted and
debunked the moment he thought them. Some romantic
idea of Eastern and Western influence as one unified force,
which may or may not have entered Jasper's mind as he
stood in this room—some global conglomerate of ideas or
code of governance—was a fiction. The entrance of Japan
into the equation was merely the influence of its arts of
self-defense, ninjutsu, the serrated edge to a military tactical
knife manufactured by the West.

If the West could steal a little bit of forethought, of style
to inject into its weaponization, so be it, they would steal it,
and steal it mightily and without apology. There was no
romance here; such a notion amassed to nothing greater
than a delusion. Perhaps a great delusion, but a delusion
nevertheless, he thought.

Jasper and Paris paced around the perimeter of the
sunken room and perused the various weapons it exhibited.
They selected their desired items—

Shuriken [throwing spikes];

Kusari Fundo [short length of chain with weights on the
ends];

Shuko [hand spikes/claws];

Ashiko [foot spikes/claws];

Tessen [spiked iron fan];

Kyoketsu Shogei [spear tip and sickle attached to a long
chain, an iron ring at the end; the use of this weapon wasn't

immediately clear, but it would no doubt fuck someone seriously up];

Tanto [short knife with wooden handle];

Kodachi [short sword];

and a grappling hook.

As Paris lined up the cache of weapons across the floor in order of their respective sizes, Jasper cataloged them in his notebook. He even went so far as to sketch each one of them out, in an effort to enhance the clarity of his list.

"What are you doing?" Paris asked.

"Inventory," Jasper responded, looking up from his notebook.

"This isn't a sporting goods store."

"I'm done." Jasper closed his notebook and slipped it into his pocket.

Paris shook her head and began packing the weapons tidily into a surplus of duffle bags. While they may not have admitted to having much in common as father and daughter this early into their reunion, their shared attention to detail, and reverence for artillery, was sufficiently evident.

The landline in the apartment began to ring the sound of an out-of-date digital beep, beep, bee-beep, beep, beep.

"Who would be calling here..." Chauncy muttered.

Jasper placed a hand on the side of Chauncy's shoulder, interrupting him—he got it, and got it quickly.

Jasper rushed back up the latter, taking two rungs at a time, retracing his steps through the closet to the living room. He quickly discovered the source of the sound: a portable phone resting atop a battered thesaurus. Both sat on the coffee table. He picked up the phone, "Hello?"

On the other end of the line, Blythe drove frantically through the belligerent San Francisco streets, talking rapidly into a Bluetooth headset.

"I've been made," she said.

She squinted nervously into her rearview mirror, as if someone was tailing her, before glancing back down at a GPS monitoring device affixed to the dash.

"We need to connect and we need to connect now."

The device beeped, and it beeped faster the closer she got to Jasper's location. The beeping was faint, but Jasper heard it clearly enough through the holes in the handset. He took a second, keeping the phone to his ear, and looked around the living room, noticing the stillness in the apartment.

"How did you get this number?"

Blythe cut off the car next to her, a prehistoric Saab with a handful of miles left in it. Its horn blared in the background. Jasper pulled the phone away from his ear.

"Fifteen minutes," she said.

"Are you monitoring me?"

"I had no alternative."

"Fifteen minutes," he responded, a bit flustered.

"See you soon."

Jasper hung up the phone. He searched his pockets and found the dime-sized metallic object in his coat pocket. It felt extra heavy; a weight that accrued while holding it. It was blinking. He stared at the blinking.

***

Not even ten minutes later, Jasper and Paris stood at the side entrance of the club, both shouldering equal burdens of duffle bags. A few delinquent skateboarders practiced their ollies at the end of the alley—mostly failed attempts, but that didn't stop them from risking sprained ankles and broken wrists to get it right. Blythe's car pulled up to the curb before any ollies were actually landed.

Jasper opened the back door as Blythe met eyes with him, giving him a quasi-reassuring nod, which he accepted and then passed along to Paris. Paris glanced at the skater-punks; there was something free and reckless and reassuring about their quixotic leaps and kicks and plants; there was something, perhaps, more reassuring than what Blythe had to offer inside this car. But she didn't have a choice. Paris couldn't turn back now. She was in too deep. She just didn't realize how deep, until such a choice—or lack there-of—introduced itself.

Paris hastened into the backseat, Jasper closing the door behind her. He opened the front passenger side door and hopped into the vehicle. Blythe shifted the car into drive and sped away down the street, the landing of ollies left to linger in the category of the unknown.

"D.I.C.?" Jasper asked.

"Yes," Blythe responded. "They were all over me."

Blythe, eyes glued to the rearview mirror, turned down a side street that was sandwiched between a series of alleyless buildings.

"I must be getting close..." Jasper twisted into the back, looking at Paris, "to finding her."

Paris looked away from him; she didn't know what to believe anymore.

About halfway down the block, a lone fire truck ahead of them changed lanes, flipping on its swirl of lights as it pulled in front of them. It then braked abruptly.

Blythe, whipping her eyes away from the mirror, cut the steering wheel and swerved sharply and severely to her right. The uneven curb sliced through her front tire—her rim scraped violently against it. The damage wasn't nearly enough of an impediment to slow her car's thrust, causing her to crash into the back of the massive municipal vehicle. Blythe and her passengers were projected forward.

Despite some whips of the neck, no one inside the car was hurt. Just shook up, on the outside; there wasn't much left to shake on the inside.

Another fire engine, with its own set of spinning lights, proceeded to pull up behind them, nudging up against Blythe's back bumper and blocking them into this valley of buildings and trucks.

"Let me handle this," Blythe said, her hands trembling, evincing what William Burroughs might have described as *the copper jitters*. The context here, however, was completely different. It was the paranoia that was the same.

She reached for the door, opening it into the unfamiliar street. As she put her foot to concrete, Jasper grabbed her arm.

"You're too important," she said, shaking her head at him.

Jasper continued to hold onto her, and it was a viselike grip.

"Jasper, I need you to stay here."

Jasper finally did let go of her arm, against whatever judgment he could fathom as better and just.

Blythe stepped outside the car, closing the door behind her. As she cautiously advanced toward the truck in front of her, two masked men in dark attire emerged from the mammoth sides of the vehicle—they did not look like they were employed by the city. Blythe stutter-stepped, before ceasing her stride altogether.

Jasper could only watch; he couldn't hear any words, if words were indeed being exchanged. He watched as Blythe raised her hands into the air in what appeared to be a gesture of surrender. Perched on the edge of his nerves, he watched as the men advanced toward her.

The men advanced, but as he would soon come to realize, they weren't advancing toward her. They walked right on past her, ignoring her presence entirely. Blythe continued forward, dropping her arms to her sides as she stepped up onto the truck.

One of the men produced an assault rifle from his side and pointed the gun at Jasper. "Stay in the car," the man shouted.

The muffled sound of hissing was preamble to the murky gas that began to seep out from the car's air-conditioning vents. Jasper glanced at the gas being dispersed as it steadily accumulated into a cloud hanging above them.

Panic radiated through Paris, through her limbs, her fingers, her nails; she imagined the gas in the air burrowing its molecules into the pores of her skin. Instincts took over. She grabbed for her door handle. It was stuck, it wouldn't budge—it was as though it was soldered shut. She leaned toward the other door, gave that one a try. Same problem.

"We're locked in," she said.

Jasper looked through the windshield at Blythe, as she opened a door to the truck and disappeared into its red paint and chrome guts.

"Shoot the windows!"

Jasper slowly raised his hands in his own gesture of surrender, pressing the palms of his hands against the inside of the windshield so the gunman could see them. Paris was dumbfounded at what she was witnessing unfold before her.

"Stay in the car," the gunman shouted, "or I'll detail the interior with your brains."

Paris's rapid breathing was becoming more than just rapid.

"If they wanted us dead, they wouldn't go to all this trouble," Jasper said to Paris, trying to be as comforting as he could in this situation. Paris, visibly woozy, began sliding down in her bucket seat. Jasper reached into the back, took his daughter's hand into his and looked her in the eyes.

Their locked gaze became more and more obscured as the smoke thickened, until Jasper closed his eyes, drifting into unconsciousness.

CHAPTER NINE

IT WAS predawn at Fisherman's Wharf; a purplish hue reflected off the water, transferring the hint of outer space, the depths of some ancient and unknown nebula below its surface. It was as though the universe had been reversed. The sun was barely out, but the portion of the star that was present was enough to imply an eternity of light for which mankind would not be present to see. The enormous fire trucks, seemingly averting what little light existed around them, escorted a tow truck hauling Blythe's car across a loading dock to a waiting ferry, on which there were no other passengers. The vehicles boarded the ferry in prompt and unified succession, and then it departed.

The boat drifted into San Francisco Bay, the sun rising on the horizon, casting the beginning of its orange glow onto the Golden Gate Bridge. At this time of day, it was impossible to tell whether the vibrancy of the orange structure was a result of the light or the paint.

Light that is visible has a wavelength in the range of about three hundred eighty nanometers to about seven hundred forty nanometers, which rests in between the spectrum of invisible infrared and invisible ultraviolet light. At the lower end of the light spectrum, electromagnetic radiation becomes invisible to humans since its photons no longer have enough individual energy to cause a lasting molecular change in the human retina. This change activates the phenomenon of vision.

While light is what allows us to see, there's so much of it that we don't see; illumination is life, yet our lives are not illuminated. The *Illuminati*—plural of the Latin, illuminatus, meaning *enlightened*—was, and perhaps remains, a society that sought to bring things to the surface. These *things* may be truth, or by some accounts, the opposite of truth. It is perhaps ironic that the modern perception of The Illuminati conjures ideas of secrecy, of vagueness, of clandestine conspiracies that spider into the uppermost ranks of civilized society.

They are, or were, purported to perpetrate intricate plots outside the spectrum of visible light, the kind of light the eyes of the masses do not absorb. The information is indeed there, it's simply outside of their grasp. Jasper knew this spectrum of light existed and he was quite sure that it was in someone else's grasp.

***

Bainbridge Island. Ten miles off the coast of Seattle in the Puget Sound. Twenty-eight square miles of quiet streets, enormous lichen-wrapped trees, and a considerable mist in the air. The channel itself stretched one hundred miles, linking Deception Pass in the north to Olympia, Washington in the south. The motorcade of fire engines escorted the truck towing Blythe's car up *Burroughs Lane*, a ramshackle road adjacent to a modest farm on the outskirts of nothing close to resembling a town. A plethora of well-groomed apple trees encircled the wooden farmhouse, on which a timeworn sign read:

TREE OF LIFE APPLE ORCHARD

Jasper focused on the insides of his eyes—all he could feel was inflamed lids wrapped over viscous tissue. He felt as though he had been attempting to open them for hours, days, maybe even longer. Then it occurred to him, the years may have felt like minutes and the minutes may have felt like years, but to acknowledge either continuum would have been pointless. Whatever state or condition he was in, it was out of his control.

When he was finally able to open his eyes, however many minutes or millennia it may have taken, he discovered his body hanging upside-down in the middle of a giant cylindrical shaft. This thing was the size of an industrial wheat silo.

Jasper tried to turn his head, albeit slowly, to take in his surroundings, but he was immediately struck with a most intense pressure inside his eyes. Each time he attempted to twist his neck, his eyes pulsated. It was vicious, his heart blasting blood into his ocular passages. He was judicious in his movements, but it didn't matter. With each subsequent heartbeat, Jasper was witness to the capillaries in his eyes growing more and more red; with each heartbeat, his vision imprisoned behind a cage of blood vessels.

After a little while, the more he blinked and turned, the pain and discomfort mercifully lessened. He found he was able to twist, turn and glance around, and each time he shifted in this fashion, he was able to do it faster and more efficiently than his prior attempt. He tucked the tip of his chin into his chest and began inspecting his body. He could see that he was wearing a white undershirt, which was sopping with his sweat. His trousers and calfskin ankle boots remained firmly in place; however, his arms and legs had been bound together with nylon ratchet straps. Moreover, his head had been shaved completely and electrodes had been fastened around the circumference of his hairless scalp. While he couldn't see this, he could see the wires descending from the obscure space above him and weaving their way to his head. What Jasper imagined to be true was not far off from what was happening.

He blinked rapidly at the entirety of his surroundings: the walls of this shaft comprised of LCD screens, hundreds of them—a crystalline and perfectly symmetrical web of electronic mirrors. There was a monotonous hum in the room, a monotony that didn't last that long, ultimately, as it was disrupted by an abrupt electrical surge—it sounded like a thousand laundromat washers, their spin cycles in precise sync—and followed by a firecracker of a flash and the face of Cary Bryan—

Cary's visage appeared on each and every one of the electronic screens in a single simultaneous assault on the senses.

"Hello, Agent Robertson..."

Cary's voice echoed through the colossal chamber. The resonance, to Jasper's ears, was markedly unnatural. As his one-time colleague spoke, his face remained on some of the screens, while dematerializing on others, and then proceeded to bounce to different screens, materializing, dematerializing, and materializing again, generating a kaleidoscope of pixelated facades around Jasper, enveloping him with his personage.

Jasper, having been physically sedated, and heavily at that, tried his level best to focus on the images surrounding him and the words being disseminated along with them.

"Welcome to the brain hotel," Cary said.

"My name is…Jasper."

Jasper was confused, and he couldn't hide his confusion. He blinked his eyes more rapidly as the blood in his veins continued to rush to the floor of his skull's ceiling.

"Look around, Agent Robertson, we are inside your head."

Jasper took a cursory glance around the room, casing the place, looking for the exits, just as his training—he could only assume—had taught him to do in this type of situation. Wherever the instinct was coming from, he knew he must take full advantage of it—and exploit it to its fullest extent.

"Where is Paris? Blythe?"

"They're safe."

Jasper looked up, farther up than before. Perhaps it was the painful pulsing in his head that masked his vision previously, but he had not seen what he saw now. Above him, on a grated catwalk, two lab technicians tended to elaborate monitoring systems and jug-like receptacles of liquid. One of the techs injected the liquid, presumably some form of medication or anesthetic, into an intravenous tube that ran down the length of the harness attached to Jasper's ankles, which snaked around it like unkempt ivy and ended in a catheter attached to the side of his calf.

"You built one of these," Cary said as he produced Jasper's notebook and began flipping through it, through his research into the Dreamachine. "A version of it, at least." Cary smiled as he looked at the sketches of the geometric shapes—the Ishmaelite Archetypes—that Jasper had drawn in the pages. "I can assure you the sophistication of this particular system is well beyond anything you could possibly imagine."

Jasper felt himself going under, his eyelids getting ludicrously heavy, even heavier than they were just moments before. He began to slur his speech: "Where is my wife? Where's Cynthia?"

Cary's image faded from each of the screens, each pixel burning out in random firework-fizzling-out fashion. The walls began to shift, spinning around the circumference of Jasper's body, and the now black LCD screens began to strobe, transforming into individual panels of bright white light, blinking in hypnotically rhythmic patterns.

Jasper was hanging upside-down, like a hunk of meat in a vertical meat locker, inside of a giant *Dreamachine*.

It was a Frankensteinian version of the once simple device. Its arrangements of light bounced wildly off the outsides of Jasper's eyelids; there was no immediate rhyme or reason behind these meticulous compositions of luminescence.

Jasper couldn't help but think about just how much went unseen, and how much at this very moment remained hidden, lingering beyond the realm of his retinal scope. His body began to tremble; not because of some physiological reaction in his musculature, but because he was simply re-acting the same way the floor was reacting to the increasing rumble. The floor, itself, was shaking. The resonance of the sound was not dissimilar to how his heartbeat sounded to his inner eardrum when amplified by the pressure in his eyes. But the resonance was constant.

It was hard to put a finger on what the sound was—this sound of sound—until it occurred to him that he had heard this sound before. He had heard this sound on a daily basis. He had heard it on his television, on his radio, on his cell phone; and it was the sound of *static*.

Perhaps the most unspecific sound in the history of sound, and to the disappointment of our ears, the vagueness of the word doesn't offer any insight. In spite of that, its resonance is specifically recognized, and usually ignored, by almost every individual on the planet. We know static when we hear it, and we'll do anything to either make it stop, or avoid listening to it.

The rumbling in the room increased in volume. Jasper craned his neck backwards, leveling his forehead with the floor far below him. He blinked, moistening his burdensome eyelids, as he began to make out some detail in the floor: it looked like a giant exposed speaker that stretched to each end of the circular room like wall-to-wall carpeting, but it was curved rubber, not shag. It was hi-fi flooring. If he were to fall onto it, it might propel him back to where he was hanging like some kind of sonic trampoline. He was able to discern the details of this speaker because he was beginning to hear breaks, little slices of silence, interruptions in the deluge of static he was being exposed to. The sound seemed constant on the surface, but underneath, it was broken—what Jasper thought he was hearing were *beats*.

Out of the darkness above, came the light; out of the static below, came the beat, and the beat was upon him.

Jasper's mind was reeling as he tried to make sense of it all—tried to make sense of the senses. When he was a kid, or so he remembered, his favorite movie was Walt Disney's *Fantasia*. This was a favorite of a lot of kids. It wasn't unique in that regard, he realized. Jasper wasn't even sure whether this was his memory or Sam Robertson's memory, and in either case, if it was a real memory at all, but what his senses knew to be unquestionably real was the sound of Stravinsky's *The Rite of Spring*.

It was perhaps his earliest memory, watching that movie. Even more curious was while he could remember the sound without the image, he couldn't remember the image without the sound. It was the sound that stuck; it was the sound that placed him in the past; it was the sound that remembered the image.

Several months ago, Jasper designed a website for a classical music streaming service, a service that encouraged user interaction. He spent a lot of time on the site's forum pages, going so far as to generate a series of topics and write a number of entries himself. One of these entries focused on *The Rite of Spring*. In fact, if Cary had flipped to the earlier pages of his notebook, he would have come across his research, which was extensive. Jasper had noted that Igor Stravinsky paved new ground with *The Rite of Spring*. His composition was so new, so untested by ears, when he premiered it in Paris in 1913 the crowd rioted and attacked the orchestra.

The sounds were cacophonous, intentionally designed to be dissonant. Stravinsky had invented the discordant chord, the likes of which people and their ears had never heard, and he played it over and over and over again in a thunderous barrage on their senses.

The audience could not make sense of what they were hearing, so they lashed out, hissed and booed, and denounced the piece as the *work of a madman*. Stravinsky, to his credit, remained undeterred, and kept on pimping his sound to the public. He persisted until, literally, they started to like it. The same public that condemned it. This wasn't on account of modifying the machinations of his music, altering it to taste just as a cook might alter a recipe with herbs and spices; quite the contrary, it was the listeners who adjusted to the sound. Human beings are pattern-seeking machines. When we are confronted with something—as in the case of Stravinsky's *The Rite of Spring*—that appears absent of a pattern or harmony we can latch onto, our brains will find, and further implement, the structure.

The notion of *wrapping one's head around* a problem isn't just an idiom; it's a biological certainty.

The brain tunes its neurons specifically to adjust to sounds—sounds that upon first hearing, it can't quite make sense of—as a means of identifying recurring patterns. Within a year of the piece's controversial premiere, a majority of the masses found Stravinsky's music pleasing to the ears; so much so, in fact, Walt Disney incorporated it into *Fantasia*. The Rite went from riots to Walt Disney—perhaps it wasn't listeners' brains that adjusted to *The Rite of Spring*, but rather *The Rite of Spring* that adjusted the brains of listeners. The implications of this, while not the cause of the numbness developing in Jasper's bound ankles, certainly weren't helping things.

The thought of control, namely how *things* control, was at the forefront of Jasper's mind for this reason: he was not in control. However, he was acutely aware that some*thing* was in control of him. When asked about the origin of his composition, Stravinsky had said it came to him in a vision, "I saw in my imagination a solemn pagan rite: sage elders, seated in a circle, watching a young girl dance herself to death. They were sacrificing her to propitiate the God of Spring."

Jasper couldn't help but feel like this young girl, who was being watched, and controlled, by those around her. His sage elders were the lustrous LCD screens of light, and their voices, the rumbling from below.

Jasper was beginning to find patterns in the rumbling. He was beginning to follow the rhythm. It was the music that compelled Stravinsky's girl to *dance herself to death*; she did not do it willingly, that much Jasper understood from the composer's own words.

Rhythm is the king.

Rhythm is the king.

Rhythm is the king. The mind is jettisoned, relegated to court jester, when the rhythm takes the throne.

Its patterns take over, like a dictator of the nervous system: the repetition of prayer, of the word, of more than one word, of mantras, of anthems, of slogans, of breaths, of cargo trucks in reverse, of hammered nails, of oaths being sworn, of blinks and swallows, the flaring of nostrils, the twitching of muscles, a foot pumping under a table, or the tapping of fingertips, the thrusting of genitalia in the midst of a fuck, the convulsions of hiccups, the pulsing of the eyes in REM sleep, the throbbing aches and pains that grow more frequent—and more painful—the older you get, the alarm that wakes the body, the body that anticipates the alarm, the alarm that sets itself over time, the words, the spoken kind, the "good mornings," the "hello, how are you's," the "awesomes" the "cools" the "right ons," the otherwise superfluous responses to the same questions over and over again, the "ums" the "uhs" the "you knows" the filler to an already nonsense-packed conversation—it's the stuff you swear to use less in conversation, but end up using more and cursing yourself for not putting more effort into learning a proper vocabulary in high school.

The heartbeat was probably the most obvious example of rhythm in Jasper's everyday life; it's the most obvious example in each and every one of our lives, yet we've been biologically trained to ignore it. It's an organ that pumps blood throughout the expanse of the human body, sixty to one hundred times per minute. Jasper could feel it, Jasper could hear it, Jasper could see it swell his chest and vibrate his veins. But throughout the majority of his days, and the totality of his sleep, he was wholly unaware of it. It was his body's most powerful muscle and he did not control it—its rhythm was in control of him.

Rhythm is the king, and the king rules the beat.

The repetitions of the seasons and the inevitably of Spring to keep repeating itself solidifies Stravinsky's *right* to it. It was as though Jasper could hear the sounds of Fall, Winter, Spring, and Summer, reverberating from the static below him. The sound and the light were beginning to merge together in some kind of brilliant cosmic sync; his brain was either adapting to it, he thought, or he was just beginning to recognize what he had been hearing and seeing throughout his years on this earth, but was too blind and deaf to perceive.

He knew what he was finally seeing and hearing, what he was recognizing: the truth.

As the mosaic of LCD screens whipped around his body, flashing lights fusing with the beats bubbling from below, a near-perfect harmony of neural connectivity blossomed in Jasper's headspace. This integration drew his thoughts, his unsuspecting memories, to the surface the way magnesium sulfate might draw the puss from a boil, or a splinter from a fingertip, in an effort to heal the skin. These memories—these *splinters*—were foreign bodies reinserting themselves into Jasper's ersatz consciousness, sliding back into the front pages of his photo albums, and they proceeded forward in rapid-fire flashes.

A constellation of shimmering light ricocheted against the outside of his eyes, faster, and faster—

—FLASH—

The same memory he experienced earlier, he began to experience once again. The one in the backyard. Paris, as a little girl, swinging from the branch of a weeping willow tree. As she spread open her folding fan, peeking innocuously over it, Jasper, about twenty years younger, walked straight toward her. He lifted her up from under her arms, draping his arms around her, and hugged her tight—

—FLASH—

Jasper, about ten years younger, sat motionless in a cinema. The entire place was empty except for the one man sitting right next to him. Charlie Chaplin's silent masterpiece, *Modern Times*, was being projected onto the screen, its glorious black and white imagery being optically delivered to its two spectators.

Jasper was thoroughly transfixed by the flicker of the projection. His eyes widened, his jaw slackened; it was as though he had been hypnotized. He shifted in his seat and turned to his right, and in the most mechanical of fashions, extended his arms out in front of him.

He reached for the throat of the patron beside him. Inches away from grabbing ahold of this man's neck, he turned his eyes away from the flicker.

Jasper froze; it was immediate.

His limp arms dropped to his sides as he snapped out of his trance. Barely shaking off the disturbance—it seemed it wasn't much of one—Jasper turned back to the screen and continued watching the movie as though he had just stepped into the theater and sat down to watch it.

After only a few seconds, he became transfixed once again—

—FLASH—

Jasper, still ten years younger, sat inside a cinema. This reminiscence was a bit different than the last. It was the cinema itself; it seemed more commercial, more corporate, probably a subdivision of a multiplex in some local mall somewhere. He slouched down in his plush seat, in almost the identical spot he had occupied previously, but this time the theater was packed to its edges.

Sitting beside him was Paris, who couldn't have been older than twelve, thirteen maybe. She was staring gleefully at the movie being projected in front of her.

Jasper passed a cardboard tub of buttered popcorn to her—she laughed, popping a dripping kernel into her mouth, between the laughs. As they laughed, together, as a family, as a domestic unit, they glued their eyes to the screen—

—FLASH—

Jasper, again ten years younger, was back in the empty cinema—the same cinema as two memories before, next to the same man as before—watching *Modern Times*. The projection of the picture halted and the lights came up.

Jasper peered back over his shoulder: he observed a small cluster of scientists in the most generic of generic lab coats filming him with what looked like a movie camera. The head scientist of this bunch, Dr. Lawrence LaLonde, stepped in front of the camera as it rolled—it looked like an older machine, perhaps even 16mm, a Bolex or Bell & Howell Filmo 70, or something just as archaic.

LaLonde began addressing its lens in a French accent, "The flicker of a projected movie is among one of many 'triggers' employed to stimulate the alpha waves in the human brain..." He made sure that he projected his voice into the direction of the looming boom microphone floating above his head—

—FLASH—

Inside the depths of a darkened conference room, on a large screen built into the wall, the footage that had been filmed in the theater was in the midst of being projected. The image of Dr. LaLonde, speaking to the camera, was magnified to three times his size as he continued to divulge his findings.

"In addition, supplementary testing has garnered wonderful results with respect to the delivery of comparable wavelength stimulation in the mediums of television, the internet, and cellular telephone transmissions."

The memory was narrow at first, focusing primarily on the screen—but then it unfolded itself, expanding to reveal a large mahogany table at which several D.I.C. agents sat attentively, observing the film reflected on the screen. Among the agents in the room were Jasper and Cynthia Robertson.

"I will go on record as saying," Lalonde continued, "our initial steps toward anthropomorphic conditioning have shown... great promise."

Jasper gazed at the screen, as the others around him scribbled an abundance of notes onto legal pads. Cynthia looked up at Jasper, trying to conceal the concern etched on her face. Jasper turned to her, tilting his head down, meeting her eyes with his, and providing a reassuring nod. On the screen, LaLonde carried on with his address—

"In addition to chemical aids..."

The camera tracked its lens past a line of chemists in a lab, hunkering over elaborate pieces of equipment—glass beakers, test tubes of all shapes and sizes, and their corresponding plastic funnels, industrial scales, along with jumbo microscopes, oscilloscopes, and a variety of other scopes of which Jasper could neither pinpoint the origin, nor comprehend the purpose.

"...that are currently being developed in our pharmaceutical wing..."

One of the gangling lab techs floated a loaded syringe over to a monkey in a cage, the creature's neck secured inside the structure by a steel brace, forcing it to face a small television set. The television, its screen positioned inches from the monkey's eyes, was recycling aggressive images of London being bombed by German fighter jets during World War II. The fact that these images were iconic did not dampen their aggression; their familiarity engendered the opposite: they felt more real, and thus more terrifying, at least to human beings watching. There was a noticeable flicker that accompanied the footage, one that appeared to have been added, as though the native flicker of the film wasn't enough—it was *effect* as *affect*—and as the primate stared at these images on the screen, the technician injected the syringe into its leg.

"...we have found that fear, the emotional response to threat, acts as a natural facilitator for obedience."

The monkey began thrashing its tiny limbs about the cage. The video on the television screen cut abruptly to a montage of graphic moving images—

Black mobs looting the stores of a flooded city; a Tibetan Monk, his robe on fire; masked men breaking into a house in the suburbs with a crow bar.

"Images of destruction, of imminent external threat, most effectively conveyed through the guise of military activity..."

National Guardsmen blocked entrances to roads, cars and orange cones having been used to set up checkpoints; men in HAZMAT suits sifting through piles of mail and cardboard parcels at a Post Office in Midtown Manhattan.

"...be it the news of an airstrike or an airborne virus."

The visage of a malnourished white man in an orange jumpsuit appeared on the screen, kneeling in front of several masked Middle-Eastern terrorists inside of a cave. It was safe to assume he was being held against his will. The lighting was harsh, high-contrast, almost chiaroscuro in its juxtaposition of glowing bits of angelic stone against the dark recesses, or geological ulcers, in the sediment around them. The image was grainy, homemade, pixelated, ransom-type-shit.

One of the terrorists wielded a hacksaw, the handle of which had been secured with duct tape, and forced its serrated edge of the blade back-and-forth against the front of the prisoner's neck until he cut through to the other side, beheading the man systematically and efficiently in just a few seconds.

"These images, coupled with a subliminal flicker, are easily transmitted through broadcasts on consumer televisions and the projections of any number of violent movies in the multiplex."

The ensnared monkey continued to stare at these images on the television in front of its face; however, it seemed to grow physically and mentally complacent to what it was seeing, after having seen it for a while. Although its head was forced into the direction of the screen, it now appeared to be watching the programming with intense focus and, what might be described as, a keen interest.

The montage of footage ended, conclusively, with the Paris skyline erupting into a succession of spectacular flames.

"This process provides the optimal conditions for viewer manipulation."

Back inside of the conference room, Cynthia dropped her face into the moist palms of her hands, pushed her chair back and staggered out of the room. Jasper, jolting up from his seat, called after her, "Cynthia..."

Several agents who were standing at the back of the room, stationed in its corners, witnessed Cynthia's outburst. One of them whispered something unintelligible into a wrist-comm.

"We've also discovered that genetics may factor into repeat conditioning, administered through the eyes, allowing for the duplication of the process onto others who are predisposed to receiving it..."

Jasper glanced back at the screen: LaLonde hunched over a cage of baby monkeys nursing the nipples of their strapped-in mother as it continued its lost stare into the screen of the television.

"...as the offspring of the subject often share similar brainwave patterns."

Jasper couldn't take much more of it either; he stood up, pushing the back of his chair as far away from him as he could, slamming it against the wall, and followed Cynthia out of the conference room—

—FLASH—

Jasper chased Cynthia into the hallway: "Cynthia?!"

As the presentation continued without them present, Cynthia stomped down the corridor—if she was aware of Jasper following her, she paid absolutely no mind—brushing the shoulder of another agent as she barreled her way through. She turned the corner, leaving Jasper alone with the agent, locking eyes with him—

—FLASH—

On the linoleum floor of a decrepit gymnasium, a select group of D.I.C. agents, indistinguishable from mercenaries, practiced a regimen of ninjutsu assault and self-defense techniques; executing punch/block/kick combos in near perfect unison. Jasper was among them, performing the concentrated routine.

At the front of the gym, a Japanese man, dressed in jet-black silk robes, supervised his students. It was hard to distinguish the identity of this man; the memory was embedded deeper than most, and it was clear that it was unclear. Experiencing, or re-experiencing, his wife's reaction to the experiments had shaken Jasper straight to his core.

It had almost pulled him out of this waterfall of recollections.

Almost.

But just as the mercenaries in this particular memory were exhibiting an almost superhuman disciple in their ritualistic practice, the patterns being forced upon Jasper again took over.

Pieces of the back of this silk-robed man, this de facto supervisor, permeated the architecture of Jasper's consciousness as he marched from one student to another inside the gym. Doctor LaLonde entered the scene and approached the faceless instructor, conferring with him, albeit briefly. As they nodded at one another, forged in a form of agreement, the instructor eagerly turned toward Jasper, revealing himself to the hilt in his memory.

It was Hiroshi Ito—

—FLASH—

Jasper jogged atop a treadmill singularly housed within a transparent thermoplastic enclosure. Large metallic tanks, each boasting tubes running from the canisters to numerous vents in the sides of the plastic walls, surrounded the exterior of this chamber like the bullets of a bullet belt on the waist of a soldier scaled up in size. Electrodes peppered the skin of Jasper's chest and temples, monitoring both his heart and brain activity, and earbuds were stuffed deep inside his ears. As the treadmill increased in both speed and slope, the tubes began pumping mist into the atmosphere of the constricted chamber.

Jasper was laser-focused within the haze, every step as precise as the next. All the while he inhaled the contaminated air around him. He cranked up the volume on a small MP3 player clipped to his belt, which blasted the escalating sound of *static* into his headphones and thus into his ears—

—FLASH—

Jasper, wearing a traditional black gi, circled a rubberized dummy inside of a dojo, or what's also known as: *a place of the way*. He shifted his feet adroitly atop the floor, a large white mat with "Koga Ryu" written in Japanese in the center. The motion of his body was unnaturally consistent, like an idle video game character waiting for its player to push a button on the controller.

It was a beautiful room, the kind where beauty is derived from simplicity. In other words, there wasn't much to it. Zen Buddhists use the term *dojo* to describe a sacred space for meditation. The dojo as a space for training—specifically the training of martial arts—is primarily a Western perception.

Perhaps, in this instance, the goings-on in this space were the treacherous merger of Eastern and Western perceptions.

The semi-translucent paper attached to bamboo grids served as its walls, which began to pulse with light in assorted spots at varying points in time. After a specific pattern of light concluded, Jasper rushed at the dummy in the middle of the room. He threw a succession of punches, landing a brutal chop to the throat, then swiftly slipped around it, putting its taut head into a sleeper hold.

After a moment, a steady strobe began pulsing the room. Jasper defaulted back to his initial shuffling, continuing to circle the dummy.

Then a different light pattern began to pulsate—

Jasper sprung into the air, executing a flawless backwards kick-flip, and then landing perfectly balanced onto one knee. He breathed deep into his lungs, hopped to the balls of his feet and readied himself in a standard assault stance.

Another light pattern pulsed from the walls of the room—

Jasper charged the dummy at full speed, weaving his arm through its left limb and behind its head, flipping the polyurethane carcass over him. Jasper back-rolled onto the artificial spine of the dummy's back, yanking its head off the ground and applying a fatal choke—

—FLASH—

An ancient man sat hunching in an interrogation room, all nose and grooves in the forehead, with deep-set eyes and pruned skin. The caged bulb of the hanging lamp above him was one push away from cliché.

The face of Hiroshi Ito poked through the darkness, leaning in toward this man, addressing him—

"What is your name?"

"William S. Burroughs."

"What is your occupation?"

"I'm an interplanetary agent, but I don't think my signals are decoding in the manner they should."

"You are a drug-addict! Can you repeat that?" Ito shouted, becoming exasperated. "A junkie wife-killer!"

"You keep saying that."

"You are a drug-addict!"

"I think you have me confused with my father."

"Your father?"

"Correct."

"The Beat writer or the drug addict?"

"Is there a meaningful distinction?"

Ito hesitated, thinking the question through; or pretending to. "Is there a meaningful distinction between you and your father?" Ito asked.

"My father once told me, 'son, I was taught never listen to a priest, a policeman, or a scientist for that matter; the only thing they have is the key to the shithouse.'"

Ito backhanded Burroughs across his sunken face. "William Burroughs never had a son."

Behind a thick two-way mirror, Jasper and Doctor LaLonde sat observing this man named Burroughs as he was being questioned. The subject spat a fresh clot of blood onto the concrete floor.

"No job is too dirty for a scientist," Burroughs whispered to Ito, smirking as the words left his mouth.

Jasper watched as LaLonde inserted a hypodermic needle into a small glass bottle, generously filling the syringe with fluid. LaLonde opened a side door, entered the interrogation room and approached Burroughs with discernible indifference—he seemed to display more reverence for the needle in his hand, than the man before him, who may or may not have been William S. Burroughs.

"Ahh, Doctor Benway, so nice to see you again…you duck-fucking quack."

Jasper tilted his head down, glancing at the bottle of medication LaLonde left atop the steel desk. He picked it up and studied the label:

TYMATROPAMINE
Class: Experimental

Jasper scanned the printed letters: T-Y-M-A-T-R-O-P… He blinked at the name and then glanced up from the container. He stared back through the looking glass. Burroughs happily offered his arm, like a kid beckoning for a piece of candy, as LaLonde injected him with a complete dose of the chemicals.

"I'm running out of veins."

Burroughs slumped down into his chair as Ito wheeled in a cart with a Dreamachine balanced on top. It was, for all intents and purposes, a slightly more elaborate version of what Jasper built in his basement. It was constructed of steel, or a robust aluminum, something utilitarian and durable; aesthetics were an afterthought, if even a thought at all. Ito pushed the contraption in front of the aging gentlemen—throughout his life, Burroughs never really aged; he had always looked as though he was a thousand years old.

If this man was William S. Burroughs' son, a son whose birth was hidden from the public, the drugs had taken a toll on his looks.

"Close your eyes and stare into the machine." Burroughs whispered to himself as he leaned toward the machine, closing his eyes. "You will start to think new thoughts."

LaLonde flipped on the machine, splashing configurations of light in the shapes of the Ishmaelite Archetypes that Brion Gysin had designed; they skimmed across the floor, the walls, across Burroughs' face. His state of mind, as reflected in the loosening of his wrinkled skin, was instantly put at ease—he had been dealt his pattern and he let his physiology succumb to it.

"You are not to disclose your agency affiliation. Understand? You have no agency affiliation," Ito instructed him. "Repeat."

"I have no agency affiliation."

"You are a drug-addict."

"I am a drug-addict."

Burroughs breathed out, into the home where peace resides: "This is precisely how those sordid apes, worshipping the light between the leaves, learned how to talk, make tools and weapons, become human and... kill God."

Ito turned toward the two-way mirror, looking directly at Jasper—

"Shut the lights."

Jasper did as he was told, shutting the lights, himself peering into the spinning Dreamachine, the center of their world, as the memories twisted, turned, congealed and revealed—

—FLASH—

Jasper's mind returned once more to his recurring dream inside of the hotel, inside Le Relais de Vieux Paris—

The dream solidified into the point of view of a man, presumably the same man, from whom this viewpoint was being derived. He approached a hotel room door. The number on the outside of the door: 604.

The man inserted a card key into the upper part of the handle and softly pushed the door open. He shut the door, locking it behind him, silently. He slinked against the wall, his gloved hands grazing against the golden fleur-de-lis wallpaper, and bent around its corner, peeking into the bedroom.

Cynthia Robertson walked from the bedroom and stepped through the open French Windows onto the adjoining balcony. Jasper approached her through the eyes of this other man, as she gazed out at the skyline of Paris. Unmistakable now, with its brilliantly shining Eiffel Tower in the distance.

She turned around, looking into the eyes of her visitor. And then she smiled at him—

He didn't smile back; he just grabbed her by the throat, squeezing tightly, digging his fingers into her neck. She retracted her eyelids, snapping them back into her head, choking on what was to be her last breath, her striking physique being pushed over the balustrade little by little.

She barely got out a word: "Stop!" Two words: "Please stop..."

Suddenly the hands released her. She caught her breath, looking into the eyes of the perpetrator with desperate relief.

"What are you doing?! This is not part of the trials!" She looked around her, panicked, her eyes darting frantically in search of something. It was as though she was trying to peer into, and subsequently through, the walls around her. "What the hell's going on here?!"

The intruder bent down, locking his gaze on the red leather of her stilettos. He removed her right shoe and cradled her barefoot, pressing the palm of his hand into the arch of her foot.

Then, with a shock of suddenness, he swiftly heaved her foot up, flipping her entire body backwards over the balustrade. She screamed, but her voice faded at a rate similar to the speed at which gravity was pulling her to her death.

The man's eyes looked downward, watching Cynthia plunge several stories to the ground. The point of view then tilted itself upwards, staring at the city skyline. As traffic screeched to a halt on the city street below, a series of explosions erupted on a succession of residential and commercial roofs. The last to go was a large modern building, igniting into agonizing flames.

The killer backpedaled into the room, sitting down on the edge of the over-pillowed bed. He reached for Cynthia's purse sitting on the nightstand. He methodically burrowed his way through its contents, opening her wallet and pulling out a business card. On the card, embossed in gold flake:

LE RELAIS DE VIEUX PARIS
CYNTHIA J. ROBERTSON
CONCIERGE

The man continued to flip through the wallet, coming across a family photo of Cynthia, Jasper and Paris, posed in front of a stone fireplace. The crinkled paper relic was wedged behind a credit card. It was stuck to the back—it had probably been in this place for a while—it was the place it was supposed to be, where it lived, within these tight quarters, whether it was looked at or not—whether it was viewed daily, or never at all—it was there, it was felt, she carried it with her.

The man's eyes held it and looked at it—and then hesitated for a moment, dropping the photo, turning toward a wall mirror—

He glimpsed the reflection in the glass: he glimpsed Jasper.

CHAPTER TEN

IT ALL came back to Jasper, as if in an instant. This image, this image of truth, unlocked it all—it was no longer just a neurograph.

He had been to Paris. He had been to Paris numerous times, in fact. Many of these times, which he didn't remember before today, he cared not to remember at all. He wished it were possible to suppress them again. Nearly every one of them he wished he could forget, except the first time he'd been there: his honeymoon.

His wish to travel to Paris with Paige was a wish that had already been fulfilled with his real wife.

Jasper—or who he was, Sam—remembered purchasing a first edition of Ernest Hemingway's *A Moveable Feast* amongst the miles of books at the Strand Bookstore in Greenwich Village as they prepared for the long flight ahead of them. *Paris stays with you*, Hemingway wrote. They took great pains to plan their trip: what restaurants to dine at, which attractions were worth waiting on line for, and most important of all, pinpointing places to relax and not look and sound like a couple of hapless tourists. The latter wasn't really a problem; they were spies, they were trained to fit in anywhere.

Nevertheless, it was nice to pretend they were normal every now and again, shifting their focus to the banal periphery of the everyday. For them, the banal was more of a blessing than a curse—a daydream, not a nightmare. The grass is always greener, so they say. For spies, this idiom is fitting.

Jasper had wanted to visit the City of Light, but it was really Cynthia and her affinity for the Parisian urban sprawl that begat their journey. There was a part of her that felt she belonged there, while never having set a sole atop its streets. She felt it somewhere inside. It's indeed interesting, but not uncommon for people. Where we are born, and down the line, where we die—are these places we're meant to be, and following that, meant to be at both the beginning and the end? Why are we born one place, while others are born elsewhere?

If there is to be a city of origin, the question is: what's more apropos than *the City of Light*?

The city of enlightenment. The enlightenment of the five senses. No other city in the world values the fulfillment of the five senses quite like Paris, France. The eyes are obvious; the eyes absorb the light. Auguste and Louise Lumiere invented the cinematographe—a combo camera, developer and projector—and it was in this city they screened the first film to flash the retinas of an audience. When the film was presented, or so it's been documented, spectators were so frightened by the moving image of a life-sized train rolling toward them that they began screaming and fleeing to the back of the theater. This ocular history, combined with the taste of the finest cuisine, and its requisite smells, the sensory pleasures, side effects inside the most romantic place on earth, along with the ears, the streets that echo with never-ending music, offered an undeniable magnetism.

Jasper could see the life, those extra ounces of life, percolating inside and bubbling to the surface of his wife as they walked the city streets. Paris as a prescription to melancholy, that seemed a novel thought. Cynthia had always wanted a child and was recently diagnosed as infertile. They still planned on getting a second opinion. The thought gave them hope.

They marveled at the city—there's much to marvel at—but they were impressed largely with its symmetry. Everything was unique, yet the same. Cynthia enjoyed a love of the macabre. Her favorite short story was Edgar Allan Poe's *The Tell-Tale Heart*, which she'd appreciated since she was a kid, and her favorite part of the story was that it was told from the point of view of the murderer. Macabre, indeed. It might seem obvious that first on her list of attractions to visit was the catacombs, or *Catacombes de Paris*, which resided deep within the bowels of the city. These underground tunnels housed the bones of six million of the city's residents, many who died in the plague and were buried in the mass graves of the Cimetière des Innocents.

One only needs to descend the stone spiral stairs, no less than six stories of them, to access the abyss below Montparnasse. While above ground the city celebrates the senses, the catacombs deprive them. As Jasper and Cynthia's eyes adjusted to the darkness, their ears embraced the sounds of gurgling and spluttering around them, presumably from the nearby aqueduct—when one sense was strangled, the others breathed deeper breaths. They walked through its winding corridors of mortared stone, crouching when necessary, as the narrowness of the space bore oppressively down on them. Jasper didn't consider himself claustrophobic, but when placed in an environment like this, he couldn't help but think that everyone was a little claustrophobic. Wasn't being buried alive a relatively universal fear?

This terrifying thought was, perhaps, amusing to his wife, considering her choice of gothic reading material. For her, romance just wasn't as romantic without an injection of a decent dose of horror.

While spending an afternoon navigating these tunnels wasn't high tea at The Ritz, the experience thrilled Cynthia. These caverns were once mined for a variety of precious stones; now they're the final resting place of some of Paris's least fortunate citizens. Jasper glued his eyes to the walls, which after his retinas adjusted, realized weren't walls at all, not in the traditional sense. These walls were built of the *bones* and *skulls* of the deceased.

Jasper couldn't help but marvel at the care that went into organizing and shelving these bones; the symmetry was something to admire. While human culture has historically celebrated the individual, the uniqueness of a single mortal being, this post-death memorial sought to preach the opposite writ large: we are all the same. Millions upon millions of bones, stacked perfectly atop each other, every piece in every row lined up with precision. It was clear that much labor went into measuring these elements—the aesthetic design of the surroundings alone was awe-inspiring—but it was also clear that not much, if any, thought went into keeping the bones of the individual together.

It was as if the entire point of this memorial, this place of rest, this tourist destination, was that death destroys the individual. From the top: a row of skulls, followed by three feet of femurs, tibiae, fibulas and humeri, followed by another row of skulls, then another three feet of bones pointless to identify by name; they were surely different, but looked identical. The stacks of bones continued on until the fragmented remains became flush with the floor.

It was art, art in design; not so much eulogizing the dead, but eulogizing death itself—there was nothing individual or unique about this spectacle, most of these people were unknown anyway.

Jasper thought about this, thought about all of this, and for a brief moment took solace in the notion. We weren't unique; we were all of these bones, buried so deep underground as to be rendered irrelevant from their time of interment until the end of time as it currently stood. Some people might see the defacement of the dead exhibited in such a display; however, Jasper saw order. Much of a one's existence is devoted to making sense of what can never be made sense of, suspending order onto a framework of chaos. This place was a tribute to just that. These tunnels celebrated the heroic challenge someone takes on the moment he or she wakes up and gets out of bed. Perhaps a little melodramatic, but the feeling was entirely human.

There's a symmetry in death that calls attention to the symmetry of the universe, a universe that at a glance appears both entirely random and completely designed. The city of Paris is a kind of microcosm of the universe, both seemingly random and designed—underground there's a symmetry of bones, while aboveground, there's a symmetry in architecture.

Take the Place des Vosges in the Marais. King Henry IV built a royal pavilion in the square and subsequently ordered the other buildings surrounding the square to mimic its style. This was one of the first examples of symmetrical urban design; Levittown in the USA and other cookie-cutter communities across the globe would follow in the near, and far, future. The architecture in The Place des Vosges utilized the same bricks, the same stone facades, steep slate roofs and long narrow windows—when you hear the term *French Windows*, these are the windows being spoken of. Cynthia had always wanted a bedroom with French Windows. She could push the panes open, step onto the landing in her silk nightgown and simply breathe in the night air.

There's a beauty in the simplest of things, and this kind of beauty was never lost on Cynthia—and when she thought it was lost on Jasper, she would make sure to remind him of it every chance she got.

Their stroll through the catacombs might have been the first time that feeling wasn't lost on Jasper—he walked past the rows of skulls, and the milieu felt welcoming, and it felt welcoming in the most non morbid of ways. That's what was strange. It felt right, everything felt in its place, not just the bones, but also he and his wife, walking through these corridors, side by side. The entire place made them aware of their insignificance—of humanity's insignificance—in such a way that made them—make us—*want* to live.

Jasper looked at his wife and he knew she felt the very same thing. Perhaps that's what she got out of Poe's writings; being introduced to death and its limitless incarnations, it brought one naturally closer to life.

Jasper and Cynthia looked into each other's eyes, into the black, as Cynthia pulled Jasper into a nearby alcove—there were lots of hidden passages down there, and visitors could easily lose themselves, willingly or unwillingly, within them. The majority of the other tourists had all but scurried past them, down the designated path, not nearly as intrigued as Jasper and Cynthia, so it was safe to say they were alone and, as far as they were concerned, out of sight.

She wrapped her arms around her husband, running the tips of her fingers up the back of his neck, digging them into his hairline. Jasper chuckled, he couldn't help it; this wasn't exactly the back of his father's sedan.

"Are you serious?" Jasper asked.

"When have you known me not to be serious?" Cynthia started laughing, too. "Come on, play along." It was a big turn on for her, that much was clear—there wasn't a single a doubt.

"Okay." And with that, Jasper kissed her. Their smiles were infectious. It was as though they were compensating for the lack of flesh to form a smile on the skinless skulls around them. It felt like these skulls were watching them, peeping on them with their eyeless eyes. They pecked at each other's lips, tugging at them, stretching the bounds of their pinkish pockets of skin. Jasper thought of his high school biology class for a split-second—a time when most every male teenager was fixated on the lips of their female classmates, among other things—he hadn't thought the lips were a part of the skin, the skin as its generally thought of when one considers the skin, but they were made of skin, an extremely thin layer of skin. So thin that the blood vessels underneath the skin showed through, giving the body part its trademark color. He found red lips—in the usual course of events—to be sexy, and Cynthia's red lips to be exceptionally sexy; ipso facto, he found Cynthia's blood to be sexy. He was attracted to it. He was aroused by it. He was in love with it. That's the most succinct way he could rationalize his fixation in this moment.

He was in love with the blood beneath her upper and lower vermillion. He was in love with the blood beneath her oral commissures. He was in love with the blood beneath her cupid's bow, the small indentation in the center of her upper lip, which he nestled the tip of his tongue into, massaging it softly on the way into her mouth.

Jasper pushed Cynthia up against the wall and leaned on some of the bones above them for balance.

"No." Cynthia said, glancing up at his hand. "Let's not do that."

Jasper dropped his hand gently to her hip as they shuffled to the center of the space. Cynthia swooped her dress under the crescents of her bottom while guiding Jasper onto the dank floor. There were small puddles of condensation scattered around them embedded into the coarse, yellowish stone, as he knelt down and mounted her. The abrasiveness of the ground was an afterthought.

The two of them made love, right there, amidst the skulls and bones surrounding them, and the fossilized remnants of prior generations of earth's creatures resting undiscovered in the rock below.

The rhythm of their love was no less symmetrical than the death that occupied the space around them. And it was perfect.

CHAPTER ELEVEN

THROUGH THE mirror, Jasper ripped his eyes away from his visage—he couldn't look at himself anymore. He glanced toward the hotel balcony, at the image of the smoldering Parisian skyline out in the distance. About as quickly as he could turn around and assess the extent of the damage, the damage disappeared. The entire panoramic setting dematerialized into the atmosphere. The only thing left where the skyline was: an enormous green screen.

Flummoxed, Jasper stood up and staggered onto the balcony. He scanned the outside, which was ablaze just seconds ago. Everything in each direction appeared to be green, as though it was painted green, or what those in the tech community refer to as chroma key green. Jasper's depth perception had been knocked askew; was the end of the green miles away or right in front of his face? It was impossible to tell. He leaned over the balustrade and peered down, several floors below, and there was Cynthia lying motionless, her body severely contorted, her limbs bending, gruesomely, in ways they shouldn't be bending, on the surface of the green concrete floor. Several EMT's rushed to her side, searching for life signs—

But she was dead.

If this wasn't apparent enough to Jasper, the glacier of blood extruding from the gash in the side of her head obliterated any doubt he might have had. Cynthia's body was defined by its blood—a red blemish amidst the bright green ground, two complimentary colors at play, flagging this memory in Jasper's consciousness, like the wistful re-membrance of colored Christmas lights wrapped around the tree as a child over the holidays.

This color combination would forever alter Jasper's psy-che—once he remembered it.

As Jasper stared down at his dead wife, agents took the room apart. The ceiling was swiftly hoisted off the walls, and the walls around him rolled away, revealing the *hotel room* as an elaborate set in the middle of a soundstage. The floor of the room was built atop scaffolding that was sev-eral stories high. Though it was a simulation, Cynthia's fall was quite real.

EMT's rushed toward Jasper, sitting him back on the bed and taking his vital signs. One EMT, a bony fellow, armed with pen-sized plungers, tilted Jasper's head back and suctioned a pair of green-tinted contact lenses out of his eyes. Jasper began to blink rapidly; it felt as though runaway muscle spasms had been triggered throughout the expanse of his eye sockets. He couldn't stop blinking. The EMT began flooding his retinas with eye drops meant to relax the muscles and soothe the membranes. It provided meager relief.

Within the reverie of this moment, Jasper recalled ap-proving this particular tech: contact lenses with nano grids, which tracked the image recognized by the eyes and com-posited layers of an altogether different image on top. In real-time, the green Jasper encountered in his line of sight was replaced with what the D.I.C. had created, in this case, a three-dimensional computer generated replication of the city of Paris and its topography. Wearing the contacts, it was a simple *find and replace* by the D.I.C.'s squad of keyboard-jockeys, and the world before you became something else, something predetermined, something wholly unlike the world you knew—or thought you knew—all this time.

Jasper, still blinking, turned to see LaLonde and Ito walk into the room. They approached and stood beside Jasper, surveying him; surveying the room; surveying the experiment.

"He's ready." Ito said, more to himself than anyone else.

Jasper gazed blankly into a portion of the green screen. His gaze remained there, for quite a while—he was unable to pull his eyes away from it. The substance pumping through his veins, whatever it was, it was colder than ice.

"La Machine De Rêve," LaLonde remarked.

—FLASH—

Back inside the brain-mapping laboratory. Back inside Jasper's head, or more accurately, inside Sam Robertson's head.

The pulsing LCD screens slowed to a halt like the final seconds of a spin on the mind scrambler at the amusement park. It's the moment when physical euphoria shifts into unequivocal nausea, which subsequently shifts into overwhelming regret. For Jasper, the regret was palpable, as his eyes slowly opened to the realization that he was responsible for the death of his wife—

He alone, with the brute force of his bare hands, killed Cynthia. The cut-up pieces of the future he had been glimpsing, he realized, were not pieces of the future, but rather fragments of his past.

"Agent Cynthia Robertson. Your wife." The walls around him realigned themselves, and Cary's image returned on the screens. "She was our liaison to the French

Division. The Beat Hotel was a front, a cover for D.I.C. Operations overseas since the fifties."

"Le Relais de Vieux Paris," Jasper said, shaking his head.

"Well, that's what it's called now," Cary responded, nodding. "Used to be a shithole. It was home to musicians and hustlers, writers, of course, after the Second World War. They didn't have a pot to piss in. There's a reason why they were called *beats*—they were more than happy to sell themselves to science, whether they were being experimented on by the government, or not. It didn't matter where the money came from, as long as it was green, and it didn't matter who gave you the hit, as long as the rhythm didn't stop."

Jasper's honeymoon wasn't the only time he had been to Paris with Cynthia. He had been there numerous times with her, but they were on the job. The trip they took themselves for their honeymoon was special, as most honeymoon trips are for those lucky enough to take them—but this was different.

Cynthia was told she could never conceive. However, despite her diagnosis, they were able to conceive on their honeymoon, in the city of Paris. Cynthia's empty womb had cast a long shadow over the future of their life together, but that shadow had been permeated, their love manifested by the conception of their daughter, her birth a testament to their bond, their connection, their destiny—it wasn't supposed to happen, but they made it so. Nature finds a way; nature always finds a way when the way is just, when the way is earned, when the way is a one-way street to the beginning of the end of the road.

In a word: Paris. The name of their child. Paris was their new beginning, and perhaps in this instance, the beginning of the end; certainly the beginning of the end for Sam

Robertson, who the more Jasper got to know, the more he was glad he wasn't a part of anymore.

The knowledge he was being confronted with was so damning and incredible to fathom, that it was accompanied by silence.

His brain attempted to impose a semblance of order onto the chaos, but this semblance of order just lead to more chaos; his reality was incomprehensible to the person he had become, the person he knew himself to be, the person named Jasper—with every beat of reality rang the pang of regret.

He could hear it through the quiet. He could hear each ripple of consequence that emanated from the decisions he made and had been forced to make. Sound waves need air, water, organic phenomena, but light travels alone. And the light was the master he bowed to. Nothing more, nothing less.

He retreated into his wife's empty womb, as it was before, before he killed her. It was a time when there was nothing but love between them. There, he embraced the silence. The silence of *the before*. There was comfort in absence before there was actually something to lose. The images of his past, of his crimes, had been burned into his retinas—the trauma the light had inflicted upon his soul was irreversible, but perhaps, the sound, he could ignore.

We often equate the concept of fullness with our eyes, or taste, or touch, or smell, but that's not how we consider sound; sound is about silence, absence; it's the silence that wraps itself around the content.

Sometimes it's harder to hear the truth, than to see it. The only thing Jasper could hear at this moment, in the ear of his mind, was his daughter's name.

"The agency enlisted a number of artists back then, experimental drug-testers, more than willing to test the effects of mind-expanding pharmaceuticals and stroboscopic light on the brain. The 'Dreamachine' Burroughs wrote about—it was an early government prototype." Cary gestured his hands toward the massive, and infinitely intricate, wall of screens around him. "The prototype for this."

Jasper tried to twist himself away the madness, but he could not; he was bound too tight, and there was nowhere to turn to. His upside-down remains were lowered from the ceiling as the massive speaker retracted into the ground, its rubberized peaks and valleys being covered by another floor, which mechanically protruded from the sides of the room, a floor that Blythe started walking on as she entered and approached Jasper.

Jasper immediately locked eyes with her, like a missile locking onto its target, as he was brought to her eye-level. He stared at her, upside-down.

"I'm sorry, Jasper."

She actually seemed remorseful, but Jasper could see through it—all he could see was artifice.

"You must understand, we didn't do this to you. You are, unequivocally, the product of the D.I.C.," Cary said. "They built this 'machine' to sync you up with them—with their protocol, with their purpose, with their modus operandi. They're capable of manipulating you; triggering patterns they've predisposed your brain to follow. They can make you do anything—anything, and everything, they want," he paused, "like killing your own wife."

"Bullshit," Jasper muttered.

"No, it isn't. You know what is? The life they created and hid you away inside of for years."

"Who do you work for?"

"Apple Farmers." Cary said, smirking, "That's unimportant. The important thing is how valuable you are to them. And how valuable your daughter is."

Cary's face dematerialized on the screens; and just as soon as he did, he physically materialized on the metal catwalk high above Jasper. The sounds of the soles of his shoes were all but an invitation to look up. Jasper craned his head, digging his chin into the top of his chest, to get a look at Cary standing over him. The pain in his neck was acute; he could barely roll his head around, but that didn't stop him from absorbing the surroundings he could see.

The walls began to spin again, this time merging together to become one enormous screen, and on it appeared a feed from a security camera: real-time video of Paris, pacing inside of a concrete cell.

"Your daughter's brainwaves are analogous to your own," Cary said. "According to D.I.C. records, you never had any children. She'd been completely erased from your files. But our intelligence suggested something different altogether. It was a bit of a risk, but the payoff was well worth it, I think—you led us right to her."

Jasper stared into the mosaic of screens; he was distraught, as a more than subtle sense of recognition dawned on him.

"The technology, research and development that the D.I.C. used to map the architecture of your mind, we can—quite simply—apply to your daughter. And given her age, and their advancements in this tech, she's a great deal more useful to them than you are."

"Go fuck yourself."

"You can't escape who you are, Jasper," Blythe said.

"You are a machine," Cary said. "A weapon."

"And so is Paris," Blythe added.

"We need your help to guide her, to train her," Cary said. "If you really think about it, isn't it every little girl's dream to take after her father?"

The sentiment hit Jasper like a blunt arrow to the temple. "You're gonna have to kill me," he said.

Cary, blustering with self-confidence, "We're not going to kill you. If you don't help us, we're going to kill her."

"Cary…" Blythe interrupted, taken somewhat aback. She turned to Jasper. "Jasper, I urge you to play ball here. The people we work for, they hold your entire world in their hands. There's no limit to their reach. Their influence extends from the poorest in the country to those in the very highest ranks of the government."

"In other words," Cary said, "everyone who has a television set and a prescription for antidepressants."

Jasper glanced up at Cary, standing alongside his lab technicians, as they monitored his brainwaves on a mountain of desktop computers.

"I didn't want this to happen the way it's happening, but you have to understand," Blythe implored, "this is bigger than us now…"

Jasper's eyes widened, the muscles in his face tightened, the blood pumped through his human veins with a velocity that was alarming. The words that reverberated out of Blythe's mouth and shaped by her lips were a succession of nothings, of didn't matters, of been theres, and unfortunately, done thats. The coordinated assassinations of Kuwait's Minister of Energy, Jawahir al Azzam, the fundamentalist cleric in Turkey, Hashim al Basir, Indonesian prime minister elect, Cahya Buana, and Igbo African tribal chief, Amadi Obi, were on his hands, along with a number of systematic plots to destabilize, and in some cases dismantle, those who disagreed with his makers. He had heard it all before, and had once been a willing recruit, and it was that willingness that would determine the outcome of the rest of his life.

They had built this—this *machine*—to stimulate the alpha waves in his brain, and subsequently sync them up to their patterns. The grim result was they were able to influence him, to trigger the patterns they had pre-mapped in his mind, to operate him as though he were a remote-controlled drone.

"The people that did this to you erased who you were. They blinded you from yourself. But now your eyes are open, we have new backers, and we're opening up shop again."

Jasper was a pattern-recognition machine, as all human beings were—that was the fundamental principle behind The Human Programme, the program that Jasper helped spearhead. *The Rite of Spring* was to Stravinsky as Jasper was to the Department of Information Control. It was quite simple, Jasper was the D.I.C.'s masterpiece; they composed and conducted him, time and time again.

Fact: humans seek out patterns—whether it's a pattern of stars in the sky, an attempt to decode a holy text, or the genetic mutations of this generation that mutate into the next, and into the next, and into the next. Fact: humans crave repetition, because rhythm is the king. Fact: humans are pattern-recognition machines. Fact: parents pass down their genetic traits to their offspring. Fact: Paris's brainwaves were susceptible to this technology, just as Jasper's were. Fact: Paris could be trained to do what Jasper was trained to do. Fact: Jasper was not going to let this happen.

Jasper looked around, eyeing the high-tech equipment making the monstrous steel veins of this Dreamachine pump. As the lab technicians perched above him prepared a syringe of chemicals, he could feel his senses heighten, like those of a caged animal. "You're just a bunch of hired mercenaries who don't want to get your own hands dirty," he grunted, contracting his fingers into fists, and then releasing them, stretching his knuckles out.

Cary gritted his teeth, done with dispensing the niceties, "We would like you to cooperate."

The technicians injected their cocktail of chemicals into the tube running down the harness attached to Jasper's calf. As Jasper hung there and watched, he began to slide his right foot slowly over his left ankle.

"After all," Cary snickered, "I'm no expert in human conditioning." He took Jasper's notebook and tossed it below. It floated past Jasper, coming to rest on the floor a few feet from his head.

Jasper stared at the notebook. Just as he had killed the person who he thought was his wife—the person from whom he revoked the right to live, with a seemingly insignificant jerk of a chain no more than a few days ago—his well-trained body went into action. Before that moment, he couldn't understand what was happening to him, nor grasp what he was capable of. Now, he knew, he knew everything he needed to know, and there was no need to write it down. His emotions had finally caught up with his physical metamorphosis.

He was like those growing toys he had given Paris as a child. They called them *grow monsters*. Put them in water and grow them up to a hundred times their original retail size. Paris had an octopus; she loved that octopus, even though it was nothing more than a superabsorbent polymer in the shape of an octopus. It was made of the same stuff used to manufacture disposable hygienic products. Jasper remembered giving Paris a dropper, which she used to experiment on the toy, intermittently releasing drops of water onto it, reanimating it one tentacle at a time.

Once the monster was fully grown, it had the ability to be dried and shrunk back to its retail size so it could be played with again.

The water had been released onto Jasper, reanimating him intermittently over the past few days, months, maybe even years. His molecular form was no different than Paris's grow monster—polymers, blood and guts aside. The only difference was, in this case, there would be no shrinking him back to his retail size.

He slipped his toe into the side of his opposite boot and pushed a hidden tanto—his short knife—through the inside of it, puncturing its rubber sole until it reared its razor-sharp tip on the bottom side.

"But, you're right..." The chemicals continued to stream down the tube as Jasper wedged the blade against the harness from which he dangled. He began to saw back and forth at the binding, "...I am an expert," and then kicked, digging the knife into the double-layered nylon and snapping the straps—

Jasper flipped to the floor, the intravenous tubes and electrodes ripping off his body as though they had barely been attached to him. He landed firmly on his feet: face-to-face with Blythe.

While the notion that you're not who you thought you were, that your memories may, in fact, be a fabrication, may be horrifying to most people, the life-altering conclusion that you're a blank slate is not an accurate assessment: the body remembers, the muscles remember, the limbs, the fingers, the toes, the genitals remember, often to the mortification of whatever's left of the mind.

Jasper was no exception: Jasper remembered.

He noticed a tear dripping from Blythe's eye as he looked at her, traversing the hill of her cheek, just before he kicked the bottom of his boot into her neck. Her eyes

retreated into the back of her head, not so much in surrender, but in inevitable and immediate demise. There was
remarkable gracefulness to the move. It seemed choreo-
graphed; it seemed rehearsed—choreography that Blythe
was never taught, of course, nor had occasion to rehearse
herself.

Jasper removed his boot, extracting the tanto from her
jugular vein, releasing an eruption of nearly a third of the
blood in her body. The corporeal remains of Blythe
deflated limply to the ground.

Jasper whipped his leg up, pulled the bloody knife from
his boot and cut into his wrist restraints, slicing through the
nylon like it was scotch tape. He stood over Blythe, for
what would no doubt be the last time, and watched as the
blood depleted, a broken hydrant on the curb of a dead-end
street.

CHAPTER TWELVE

ALARMS ECHOED as stalactites of red light swirled on the ceiling. Cary peered down from above at his fallen comrade, the blood still bucketing out of her body. Before Jasper could look in his direction, Cary rushed off the catwalk, disappearing into the innards of this complex that were as familiar to Jasper as a rat in its first maze.

Regaining control of his focus, Jasper observed the floor. He had once been familiar with this place, he knew that much. But, thus far, that assumed familiarity had not bubbled back to the surface. Not completely, anyway. He glanced at his notebook, a missive that wore the camouflage of Blythe's blood; it was a part of the carnage that covered the floor, a part that would remain there along with the other dead parts of his past. He looked up, never to look at it again.

As Jasper twisted around, he spotted what appeared to be a large, rectangular two-way mirror. He looked to his side at the steel examination table in the far end of the room. It was a heavy-duty piece of equipment. He shuffled over to it, got behind it with all his weight—its legs were on wheels—and started pushing it toward the glass. As the utilitarian piece of furniture gained momentum, Jasper slammed the end of it into the mirror, crashing through his reflection and smashing the glass to bits.

Jasper leapt through the jagged opening, gaining entry into the facility's observation room. As he hit the ground, he ducked into a front roll to avoid the submachine gunfire from two security guards stationed inside.

Picking up a couple of glass shards, he sprung to his feet and threw both pieces in rapid succession. He hit one guard in the neck, squarely obstructing his windpipe and releasing a current of blood into the man's lungs. He crumbled, brutally gagging on his bodily fluids, while the other man was struck bluntly in the eye.

Jasper approached the one-eyed guard on the ground. He was still alive, his twitching limbs piled atop the floor like a bag of dirty laundry—he was feebly reaching for the handgun holstered in his belt.

Bringing down the quadrangular heel of his boot onto the man's face, Jasper sent the rest of the glass through his eye, breaching the cortex of his brain, the microscopic splinters of glass splitting from its origin shard and lodging into the porous tissue of the man's frontal lobe.

Jasper reached down, rather indifferently, and relieved the man of his handgun and earpiece.

***

Ito, along with several other agents, assembled along the expansive runway of a military airport somewhere in the Southwestern United States. The expansiveness of the tarmac was only enhanced by the endless expanse of desert surrounding it. The agency's military attaché, a stout man with a graying goatee and aviator sunglasses, approached Ito. "We have an alert in sector six-zero-four."

"604?" Ito asked.

"We're gassed and ready-to-go. Prepared to proceed as directed."

The baritone roar of an engine accompanied the SX-51 Blackwing Bomber as it taxied out of an oversized hanger, which appeared as though it was the only structure on the site, "On your call, sir."

Ito leaned back, surveying the massive weapon of winged destruction as it rolled onto the tarmac—the aircraft never ceased to command the attention and awe of those with the clearance to be this close to it. He looked at the attaché, giving him a nod in the affirmative.

***

Inside a crepuscular tunnel under the ground, Cary climbed down a ladder, the facility's alarms reverberating as he secured the inside of the metal hatch behind him. The space was reminiscent of a small mining shaft, illuminated by hanging work lights suspended above, their cords bolted into the uneven ceiling. Cary's foot slipped on the last rung of the ladder, the treads of his sole sliding on a spot of grease. He dropped into the grime of the passageway, losing his balance a little and nailing his knee on the corrugated ground. He groaned before lifting himself up, brushing off his leg and scurrying through the passage.

In the midst of his stride, he grabbed the walkie-talkie clipped to his back pocket, depressed a button and barked into the device. "We need the subject alive. Shoot to wound. Repeat. Shoot to wound."

Inside the observation room, Jasper kicked the exterior door of the room open and proceeded with caution into the hallway. The alarm blared throughout the facility and spinning red lights highlighted both ends of the hall. He placed the guard's earpiece into his right ear and paused to listen. He instantly recognized Cary's voice: "Repeat. Shoot to wound."

Leaving the earpiece resting at the edge of his ear canal, Jasper continued to shuffle down the hallway. As he turned a corner, another security guard came barreling toward him, machine gun in hand—these guys all kind of looked the same, and fortunately for Jasper, they all kind of acted the same. They embodied a predictability that he welcomed.

Jasper didn't hesitate; he ran straight for the man—two freight trains on an out-and-out collision course.

As the guard raised his weapon, Jasper dropped to the ground. He slid flat across the floor as the guard discharged his firearm above him, and then propelled his foot upwards into his assailant's trigger finger, dislocating the man's knuckle and kicking the gun from his hands. Jasper grabbed onto the back of his leg—he pulled the tanto from his boot and sliced through his challenger's ankle, severing his Achilles tendon clean through the tissue.

The man collapsed, shouting out in pain. Jasper swung his arm up, bringing the crest of the knife down into the guard's chest.

Jasper hopped up and kept on moving, heading toward a bombproof steel door framed within what looked like the entrance of the place, a foyer equipped with a card reader and keypad. This thing was industrially reinforced. He tested it, grabbing a hold of its handle, but he didn't have to test what he already knew: he could not possibly force it open.

He took a second glance at the reader, then pulled his handgun and shot a bullet into its slot—after a couple of sparks, it chimed.

"Authorized," an automated voice intoned.

A series of hydraulic locks turned and unbolted as the massive door opened toward him. Jasper tilted his head at the gun, surprised it had succeeded in actually opening the door. This wasn't some movie or something—how many locks, or security mechanisms, reinforced or not, could withstand the impact of a bullet? He bet very few people actually tried shooting up one of these things before. Be that as it may, he unlocked it, and the open door revealed the outside of the property.

Jasper stepped into the sun-drenched world he'd been deprived of for however long he had been held captive. He had no idea how long he had been there. He had no idea how long his body was suspended in that machine, or how long his mind was suspended in time. He didn't care much about it—about losing track of time—not since he had lost track of himself. He grieved less and less for time the more time went on.

The exterior of the building, judging from this entrance, was dressed unobtrusively shabby, as though purposely so. It was wooden and it was rustic. The purpose seemed quite clear to him: to conceal the long sterile hallway and facilities it lead to inside.

Jasper edged toward what appeared to be a giant orchard, squinting his eyes at the sun that burned above him. Bringing his head down, he surveyed the symmetrical, and seemingly endless, rows of apple trees in front of him. He sidestepped to the corner of the building, peering around its side—

At the other end of the complex, fire trucks systematically lined up in front of a large loading dock. This particular section of the building arched; it might have been a warehouse or a storage area connected to the facility. A group of agents monitored a series of hose-like tubes running from the building and into the trucks. In addition, men decked out in fire department gear and rubber gas masks transported unwieldy tanks from the dock—massive versions of the kind that typically store compressed air—loading and securing them onto the backs of the trucks.

Jasper retracted his head back around the corner. He hugged his back against the wall as he reversed course into the other direction. The sensation of the abrasive wall sliding against his shoulders conjured images of his daughter, Paris, cast in silhouette, performing a comparable routine on the stage of the Rotten Orange—slinking against her own wall, in route to the pole, eluding and alluring, simultaneously. Apples and oranges. Father and daughter. The context of both, he wished he could forget.

As he reached the other side of the building, he peered around that corner—shots splintered the wood just inches from his face.

Jasper snapped his head backwards. He looked down near his feet, grabbed a chunk of wood siding that had broken off the building and extended it around the corner, shielding the exposure to his body from the gunman. More shots rang out, blasting the wood out of his hand and back to the ground.

He then got down onto the ground, digging his chest in the dirt. He pulled a shard of mirrored-glass from his pocket and positioned it around the corner. He looked into the reflection, surveying the side of the complex: it looked the same as the back—more apple trees. As he gradually rotated the mirror, he spotted Blythe's car secured to the bed of the tow-truck.

He thought back to his last moments in that car, to the last moment he was with his daughter, before the haze split them apart. Steadying the glass in his hand, he waited.

After several minutes, there was movement roughly fifty yards away: a small wooden panel, built into the ground, lifted a few inches. Jasper strained his focus, glimpsing the barrel of a rifle emerge through a thin space between the panel and ground. It appeared to be an underground hatch of some sort. He rotated the mirror, catching sight of two more of the panels peppered across the ground.

He turned the mirror back toward Blythe's car. He proceeded to break a slender piece of wood from the broken siding and remove some wire from a mesh covering affixed to a drain at the base of the building.

Pulling his handgun, Jasper slid the wood between the finger guard and the trigger, measuring a few inches in length. He took the wire and fastened the wood, which jutted out on both sides, to the trigger. Hefting the weapon in the palm of his hand, he unlocked the safety, wound his arm back and hurled it over the roof toward the triangulation of ground hatches.

It bounced to the ground, slamming the wood back, and engaged the trigger—firing off a round.

At the sound of the shot, Jasper booked toward the car. The hatches closed as the gun continued tumbling, like a semi-automatic tumbleweed, raking the piece of wood across the ground, firing more rounds into random directions.

Once the frenzied firearm settled itself, the rifle barrels reemerged from the ground, orienting themselves to their surroundings, catching sight of Jasper closing in on the vehicle.

The snipers attempted to pick Jasper off with a few more shots, but he was too fast for their aim; he was already behind Blythe's car. Jasper caught his breath, but it was only for a second. He opened the back passenger door, keeping his head concealed beneath the frame of the window, spotted his duffle bag on the backseat and dragged it out.

He unzipped the canvas bag, assessing his cache of weapons inside.

***

A phalanx of armored helicopters sliced through the sky, materializing from the miasma of the clouds. Inside the rock-hard shell of the lead helicopter, Ito and several black ops agents strapped on fiberglass helmets and clipped chest harnesses to drop-lines. The pilot turned, glancing backwards into the belly of the aircraft. He spoke into a headset. "One hundred miles and closing."

Ito nodded at the pilot, knocking his knuckles against the front of his helmet in acknowledgement.

Inside of the underground tunnel, Cary reached the end of the abyss, approaching a steel door with an equally robust guard standing outside of it. "Open the door." The guard unlatched the door, opening it wide.

Cary stalked into a concrete bunker—less like Hitler's bunker, more like a short-term suite at Guantanamo. In the corner of this perfectly square and monochromatic room, Paris was crouched down into something that resembled a ball. It was as though she was willing her body to recede into the minuscule cracks and crevices in the ground's atomic structure.

Cary pulled his .45mm handgun, pointing it down at her, aiming the barrel at the crown of her head.

"It's not polite to point a gun at someone," Paris murmured, barely looking up at her captor.

"Get up."

"How 'bout I point this at you..." She extended her middle finger toward him, but did so in as endearing a manner possible. Paris had surely executed this maneuver to a number of ill-tempered patrons in the course of her tenure

175

at The Rotten Orange—she performed it with panache and without apology.

Cary lunged at her, yanking her up by her hair. "Get up!"

Meanwhile, outside in the plot of the apple orchard, Jasper slowly began to stand up, his back planted against the car. He was dressed in an amalgam of Gi and G.I.—black military cargo pants; split-toe tabi boots; a black jacket with gauntlets covering the tops of his hands and forearms; and a tight black hood. He tied a black mask around his neck, chin and mouth, and tucked it into his hood, tightening the anonymity of the fabric around his face—the finishing touch.

His person was loaded with as much ninjutsu weaponry that he could physically take and manageably handle.

He raised his head, little by little, peeking inconspicuously through the portal of the passenger side window. His eyes spotted the keys hanging from the ignition. He turned toward the front hood, crawled over to the cab of the tow-truck and started unhooking Blythe's car from its grips. The bulk of the cab blocked Jasper from the snipers' view as he carried out his task.

After disconnecting the car from its mothership, he creaked open her front passenger door and crawled inside the vehicle, making sure to crouch out of sight of the windows.

He retrieved the kyoketsu shogei [sickle and chain] from his duffle bag and wrapped a length of its chain around the steering wheel, tying the links into a makeshift knot. He leaned back, pulling on it tight, making sure the chain was secure. Taking a handful of bullets from his pocket, he hastened to remove their tips and began sprinkling their gunpowder innards along the dash and onto the floor.

He reclined the driver's seat and started the car. Realizing he only had what was, in real-time, just a few seconds, he kept his head down and made an effort to, effectively, trick his mind into perceiving the world in slow motion, into being one step ahead, as being caught one step behind would likely result in his death. He wrapped his fingers around the ball of the gearshift and put the car into reverse, rolling down the riveted bed of the tow-truck and skidding the vehicle into drive.

Gunshots peppered the glass as Jasper accelerated toward the hatches, the source of the enemy fire.

As the car fiercely gained speed, closing on its subterranean targets, he jimmied a shuriken into the accelerator pedal, locking it down and hopped the center divider into the backseat. He wound his leg and kicked out the rear window, grabbing his kyoketsu shogei and leaping through the opening.

Once the driverless car hit thirty miles per hour, Jasper gripped the chain and proceeded to scale the trunk, stepping onto the bumper and then hopping onto the moving ground. The bottoms of his boots skimmed the surface of the earth as he steered the vehicle with the chain—he was like a charioteer of some post-apocalyptic, gas-guzzling chariot.

The surrounding snipers unloaded their rounds on the speeding contraption heading right for them—

Several of the bullets grazed the dash, igniting the gunpowder. The inside of the car burst into flames. Jasper let some slack out from the chain, providing a middling degree of distance between his person and the inferno that was pulling him along. As the flaming vehicle reached the center hatch, the sniper ducked inside, milliseconds before the undercarriage of the car tore the hatch from its hinges.

Jasper gripped his sickle, readying it. As the car cleared the hatch, Jasper leaned down and tomahawked his steel crescent into the chest of the sniper, locking it firmly into the latticework of the man's rib cage. Jasper let go of the weapon, tumbling away from it. The sniper grunted loudly as the chain tightened and the sickle plucked his body out of the hole, jerking the meat of him haphazardly into the air.

Jasper hopped up, sprinted to the hatch and dropped into it. Aboveground, the sniper's writhing body was being dragged along the coarse terrain as the car continued to gain speed, heading straight toward the trunk of an apple tree.

Jasper peered over the side of the hole, observing from a relatively safe distance as the automobile crashed into the tree, exploding into a smoldering fireball. The momentum of the runaway car catapulted the flailing sniper into the middle of the flaming wreckage.

Jasper scanned the area: no imminent threats. He turned and dropped back down into the hole. In doing so, he had consequently infiltrated the facility's extensive tunnel system—the web of metaphoric neurons through the brainstem of this hideous operation. Jasper's spinal cord was very much connected to the entire thing; he was a puppet, but he was a puppet who had regained the control of his hippocampus, the hard drive that stored his memories, and it was these memories that steered his body and propelled his mind through these tunnels—it was these memories that reminded him of when he once explored similar tunnels below the streets of Paris. The journey in his past, deep under the City of Light, was driven by the *love* for his wife, and the unknowable *love* for his future daughter; this journey—the one in his present—was a journey driven by unadulterated *hate*.

Jasper's brain returned for a brief moment to the initial research he conducted into the Dreamachine, namely the *enneagram* and its personality types—

The Perfectionist	One	Anger
The Philanthropist	Two	Pride
The Entertainer	Three	Deceit
The Romantic	Four	Envy
The Spectator	Five	Avarice
The Warrior	Six	Fear
The Gastronome	Seven	Gluttony
The Leader	Eight	Lust
The Mediator	Nine	Sloth

He had entered the Human Programme when Paris was 6, left her at the age of 12 and, now that she was a woman, the age of 18, he had reentered her life.

Three divisions of six, each division representative of a series of choices that Jasper—that Sam Robertson—made throughout his life, all of which directly affected his relationship with his daughter, choices that altered the trajectory of his life in unalterable ways. His existence took the form of a three-dimensional triangle. The seeds of fear had been planted in its base, destined to take root, flourish and grow upward, and over time envelop the apex of the pyramid, the unparalleled point-of-no-return, inside of which held the inescapable conclusion: he was born a *warrior*.

Whether he was an unwilling warrior, or not… well, to debate such a thing was pointless. If the mystical properties of the number 3 led him to this conclusion, his process of deduction was immaterial—the legitimacy of such a deduction was for the mystics to determine. Jasper's fundamental weakness was fear; specifically, he feared losing his daughter for the second time. While the Sufis believed the repeti-

tion of numbers, of shapes, of modes of worship, of groupings of letters, would bring them closer to God, Jasper
refused to repeat his same mistakes twice.

God was an afterthought; he thought only of Paris, and
everything that kept him away from her all these years.

The frontal lobe of this warrior was awash with revenge.
This frontal lobe of this facility—the engine that drove his
body and hoodwinked his mind for so many years—was
about to be reprogrammed, and he was going to reprogram
it, reprogramming it with his bare hands and sharpened
blades. This emboldened him, this enraged him, this en-
abled him to do what he was about to do.

Jasper pulled his kodachi [short sword] from the sheath
strapped to his back and held it out in front of him at
twelve o'clock as he advanced down the shaft.

Approaching an intersection in the tunnels, he heard the
sound of rustling in the distance. He turned to his right, a
little at a time, spotting a guard turn the corner at the opposite end of the hall. Jasper swiftly pulled a shuriken from
his cargo pants pocket and threw it, nailing his target square
in the chest.

The guard gasped for a breath as the side of his face
flattened into the ground—prompting another guard to
turn the corner nearest to Jasper.

"Someone there?"

Jasper dropped his arm, lowering a hidden kusari fundo
[short chain] from inside his sleeve. As the guard poked his
head around the corner's edge, Jasper wrapped the chain
around the man's neck and dropped to a knee—flipping
the guard over his shoulder. The guard landed on his back,
his shoulder blades slamming into the ground. He began
grabbing at the chain, instinctively, the ligaments that connected the bones in his arms, hands and fingers defending
himself, his honor, and what was left of the seconds of his

soon-to-be-short life, as Jasper brought the blade of his kodachi down into the guard's solar plexus.

***

The armored helicopters descended on the compound. As the machines hovered above the tops of the apple trees, kicking up dust and bending back branches, a rope eventually unraveled from the lead chopper and a succession of agents scaled down the line. Ito was the last to hit the ground.

He waved a finger to the helicopters above them and their spinning blades turned away, directing the crafts back toward the coast. Ito assumed the lead of the group of agents, guiding his men on foot. They removed high-powered automatic weapons from their backs—assault rifles equipped with laser sights and bayonets; a lighter, and longer, version of this accessory from combat's past. They extended the weapons out in front of them, readying them in their combat positions.

Ito stuck his hand over his helmeted head, signaling with a gesture, which prompted the squad to split apart. The men spanned out to the surrounding hatches—there were about five or six right in front of them. Without a moment's hesitation, they riddled the tops of the hatches with bullets, securing their sunken perimeters before dropping into each one of them.

As Ito surveyed the orchard, he noticed an open hatch in the distance. It was as though it beckoned to him. He released the safety on his rifle and made his way toward it.

CHAPTER THIRTEEN

INSIDE THE walls of the bunker, Cary stood behind Paris, her wrists in one hand, and his .45 in the other, which was jammed in the small of her back, right about where her tattoo was inked. He stared over her right shoulder at a small window built into the door. Through the window was the tunnel, with its sparse work lights sprinkling the area and two outsized guards pacing about.

"Bet that gun's the only thing you're able to stick into a woman," Paris said.

Cary smirked—he could not help himself, really—and loosened his grip ever so slightly. He removed the pistol from her back and slammed the butt of its handle against the side of her head.

The strike was quick and the pain was sharp. Paris hit the floor in a daze, her vision swimming in a constellation of retinal stars. As the rivulets of tears collected at the edges of her eyes, she peered up at Cary—before shifting her gaze to an open hatch in the ceiling, a good twenty feet or so above him.

From elsewhere within the confines of the tunnel, Jasper traversed the clandestine passages, studying the line of work lights streaming overhead. He followed its exposed wiring to a series of metal tubing along the wall, which ultimately lead him to a rectangular breaker box.

Readying his arms, he struck the tube running into the box with his kodachi, severing the wiring clean and disconnecting its electric nerve.

Cary's attention snapped to the window in the door as the lights in the tunnel started shorting out—each bulb zapped off, from farthest to closest, ending with the oblong fixtures of light built into the ceiling of the bunker. The room was left solely lit by the sun, which beamed radiantly down through the hatch above. The tunnel, on the other hand, remained perfectly dark.

Cary grabbed Paris by the elbow and yanked her onto her feet, jamming the gun into her flesh once again. She grunted as she tried to maintain her balance. Cary struggled to see beyond the window in the door, the span of which seemed to shrink in size each passing second; Paris, blinking uncontrollably, tried to focus her eyes on the small pane of glass, too.

Then. Suddenly. Screams. And the unsettling sounds of clashing metal.

After a rather unnatural silence, the bleeding, distorted face of one of the guards slammed against the window, his flesh stretching across the grime of the glass—it was as though his face were a funhouse mirror version of itself. At the sound of the door beginning to be unlatched, Cary began shouting, "I have your daughter. I have the barrel of my gun pressed up against her spinal column—do anything stupid, I put a bullet in it." The door continued to remain closed. "If she's lucky, she'll never walk again."

Jasper stood as still as he possibly could, just off to the side of the window, the two dead guards at his feet.

"This is your decision..." Cary said.

Jasper readied his sword, tightening his grip around its handle.

Cary pulled Paris closer to him, shoving the gun even deeper into her back—the tip of its barrel wedging itself between bone and sinew.

"...no one's controlling you."

Suddenly, a line dropped into the room. Three heavily armed D.I.C. agents slid down it as though spelunking into an uncharted cave.

Cary turned on a dime, swinging his gun toward them. Before the agents had a chance to react, Paris slithered her body under Cary's arm, gripping the appendage between her elbows. She fiercely pulled down on his forearm, breaking his elbow over her shoulder and bending his arm in the opposite direction.

She kicked at Cary's legs, sweeping them out from under him, sending him onto his back. Standing over him, she swiped his gun from the floor and pointed its barrel point-blank at his head. Her restlessness manifested itself in a slight tremble that spread through her arms and settled into her fingertips, threatening to release its growing disquiet with the swift and liberating pull of the trigger.

"Put the gun down," Ito ordered, stepping out from the darkness.

Her arm shook as she continued to aim the gun at her captor, ignoring the command.

"Put the gun down," Ito ordered, again. Paris looked up, surveying the silhouette of Hiroshi Ito, his face hidden behind the high-density plastic of his helmet. In her periphery, she detected the agents flanking his sides, each of their weapons extended forward and trained at her head. If someone were to ask, she would be lying if she said she didn't enjoy the power, the present turn of events; however, her rational mind prevailed. Her rational mind never used to prevail, or at least, not that often. With age and the most heightened of circumstances—perhaps the kind that involves your life being in grave danger—the mind can get rational real quick. She went ahead and complied, dropping the gun.

"Drop to your knees, hands behind your head."

Paris did as instructed and slowly dropped to her knees. As she lowered herself to the floor, Ito shifted his glance at the door behind her: it was open.

A shuriken cut through the air like a blow-dart and landed in the neck of the agent at the far end of the room. Jasper stepped out from the shadows in the corner directly opposite Ito, as though announcing his presence.

As the agent closest to him turned, Jasper snapped his foot into the side of the man's leg, collapsing his knee like a folding chair. As the agent crumpled, Jasper rammed a palm into his chest, sending the twirling molecules of his breath rushing out of him. Gasping for the air that recently occupied his lungs, the man spun around like a top. Jasper grabbed the agent and shielded himself with his body. He pulled his gun from behind his back and pointed the weapon at Cary. He fired shot after shot—the assault of lead he perpetrated against his former co-worker, or whatever he was to him now, seemed endless—obliterating his body with bullets.

Cary, along with any threat he may have posed, had been permanently neutralized. Jasper then turned, pointing the gun at Ito.

Ito stood stoically over Paris—he didn't seem at all perturbed by Jasper's forthrightness and aggression in his particular style of combat. "It's good to see you again, Jasper."

Jasper considered this greeting, before responding shortly thereafter: "That is not my name."

"Of course it is. I named you."

Ito removed his helmet. Paris looked up at Ito, then over to her father. The pieces of the puzzle were beginning to connect for Jasper.

"Shidoshi," Jasper said.

The two men simply stared at each other.

"I have no name." Jasper said. "Right now, I am a father—that's all I know, or care to know."

Paris could only look at her father, wondering; wondering what could have been, in a world in which her childhood was completed with him at the helm. But, the truth was, all that will ever be was wonder. And maybe that was a good thing. Maybe it's wonder that builds on the memory of absence. Maybe it's wonder that supplants the kind of memories perceived as *the bad kind of memories* that come along with growing up under another person's roof, playing by that person's set of rules, and wondering what life would be like on one's own.

Maybe wonder was exactly what it sounded like, and just maybe that sounded like a good thing.

"Whatever you've subjected me to, whatever training I've undergone, it has prepared me to die to ensure the safety of my daughter."

Jasper glanced at Paris, who could not—who would not—contain her cries, as she stared back at this man she now knew to be her father.

"Release her."

Ito didn't respond. Jasper kept his gun trained on him.

"Go, Paris."

Paris stood there, but didn't move. She couldn't; not on her own.

"Go!"

Her father's tone struck a nerve within her, that which had been embedded in scar tissue for so many years. She heard him, and she moved.

Paris ran toward the center of the room—moving the way she moved as a kid when her father called for her—and grabbed onto the rope that hung from the open hatch in the ceiling. Perhaps it's trite to point out, but this was not dissimilar to their hours spent at the playground; the actions the same, as she scaled the rope. The result might also be the same: she might never see her father again.

Ito kept his eyes glued on Jasper. Paris lifted herself through the hatch, emerging from the bunker, swinging her legs up onto the ground above. After her body cleared the opening, the square returned to the solemn beauty of its sunlit brightness, a beauty both enhanced by Paris's escape and marred by her absence. Jasper focused on the former, but couldn't help dwelling on the latter.

The moment passed as Paris leaned over the edge of the hatch and dipped her head back down into the darkness: "Dad."

She phrased "Dad" as half statement, half question, as if she was asking him if it was going to be all right, for permission for it to be all right. It was also the first time she had called him "Dad" since this ordeal began.

"I'm sorry," Jasper said. He was calm, he was content, and it washed over the expanse of his face. "Go."

Paris sprung to her feet and dashed into the orchard, brackish tears streaming from her eyes, running like hell through the maze of apple trees.

Jasper tilted his head from the symmetrical patch of light in the ceiling to the physical frame of Ito. There was, and would be, time for reverie, in this life or the next—but now was not the time for it.

"I can give you your life back," Ito said.

"I have my life back—the life you took away from me." Jasper snapped, unable to hold back his vitriol: "You made me kill my wife!"

"You understood the consequences when we recruited you."

Ito stepped forward. Jasper pulled the quivering agent closer to him, the back of the man's body flush with the front of his; he pulled out his kodachi, pressing the sharp edge of the blade to the throat of Ito's mercenary.

"I protected your daughter, just as you instructed me to." Ito snapped the bayonet off the barrel of his rifle, discarding the gun to the floor like a piece of litter. "Only I knew her identity, her whereabouts. And you made sure I hid them from you." He approached the rope hanging from the hatch, tugging on it, making it taut. He hopped up and sliced through it with his bayonet, cutting most of what was dangling. The excess rope dropped to the floor, bundling itself into a coil.

Ito squared his robust body up to Jasper, extending the tip of his bayonet out in front of him. The gesture was both welcoming and threatening. The insinuation: everything was about to come to an end.

Whether he was to meet his end or not, Jasper wasn't going to wait another second—

"You can't control me anymore..." he said, as he sliced the side of the agent's neck with both lightning speed and surgical precision, projecting a geyser of blood toward Ito. "...and you won't control her."

As the agent collapsed, Ito raised a hand to his face to block the spray of the viscous substance. The ghastly mess diverted Ito's attention, even if it was only for an instant.

Jasper moved, and moved quickly—he was physically behind Ito in no time at all. He grabbed the leftover rope from the ground, wrapped up his mentor's legs with it, and pulled hard. As Ito fell forward, he tumbled into a roll, landing as softly as soft is possible on a concrete floor.

Pivoting a knee, Ito sprang back to his feet. Jasper held his sword out in front of him, the whites at the bottoms of his eyes reflecting in the sheen of the blade—it was Ito's move.

Ito rushed toward him. They swung at each other, the edges of their blades clashing—

The two of them separated almost as quickly as their blades were brought together. They began circling each other, the concrete walls swirling behind their backs—they may have been opponents, but there was a synchronicity on display in the movements of their bodies, in this tête-à-tête of combat—

Jasper lunged at Ito again, swinging—blocking—and again—swinging—then blocking—

Once again, swinging—

Ito locked Jasper's blade in the serrated edge of his bayonet. He swiftly moved around the blade, sneaking a punch into Jasper's inner forearm, striking the pressure point of his limb. Jasper opened his hand, involuntarily, and dropped his sword. The tip of the weapon clanked to the floor. Ito swiftly jammed Jasper into a wristlock, bringing his next counter-move to a halt.

Jasper winced, the crevices all over his face folding in on themselves; the sharp pains of the maneuver rocketing from his arm and landing in the sides of his chest.

As Ito leaned his weight down on Jasper's arm, Jasper bent back and threw himself into a lopsided cartwheel, just maintaining his balance as he unraveled his wrist from the lock and kicked Ito in his lower jaw, brutally raking his upper and lower teeth together like some orthodontal buzzsaw—

Ito staggered backwards, his equilibrium having been brutally, and unexpectedly, disrupted.

Jasper threw a series of punches, each barely blocked by his opponent. But Ito managed to catch the last punch, his protégé's fist fitting into the palm of his hand like a baseball in a catcher's glove. He used the incarcerated fist to hip-throw Jasper to the ground—

This turn of event didn't last too long. It didn't last too long at all. Jasper back-flipped back onto his feet, restoring his center of balance.

As Jasper twisted around, Ito tossed his bayonet at him—Jasper flipped out of its way, somersaulting backwards, the tip of the blade chipping a jagged piece of concrete from the wall. Jasper tumbled haphazardly toward the same wall—his back hitting it hard, upside-down. He slid down the concrete headfirst, submitting to the relentlessness of gravity.

Jasper halted himself with his palms, ceasing his momentum, the top of his hood brushing against the ground.

Ito picked up Jasper's sword, and ran at him—

Jasper pushed himself from the ground, using his elbows to spring into the air and plunge his foot toward Ito—

Ito deftly slid underneath Jasper, evading his kick—

While below his outstretched leg, he swung the sword up, slicing through Jasper's gi and slashing him across the chest.

Jasper stumbled to the ground, dropping onto his elbow, as Ito's momentum skidded to a stop. He stood up, trying to shake it off, and grasped at the gash in his chest. He pulled his hand away, glancing down at it: it was dripping with blood.

Ito bent over, in what appeared to be a half-bow. It was unclear whether he was paying Jasper a form of respect or mocking him. To Jasper, it didn't matter if it was one or the other—the gesture infuriated him.

He clenched his fists and rushed his mentor as though he was immune to the pain. Ito yanked a smoke-grenade from the pocket of his cargo pants and cast it toward the ground like a football player spiking the ball.

The room billowed with smoke, almost instantaneously. Jasper continued sprinting straight ahead of him, but Ito vanished into the thick of the cloud before he could be reached.

Jasper's visibility was limited to less than a foot in front of him. The cloud was so thick he could barely see his hands—blindness descended upon him like a disease.

Ito had trained him to navigate his terrain without his eyes, to traverse the land amidst a miasmic atmosphere. Was Ito testing him again? Was he assessing his skills; specifically, whether he retained them; whether he had indeed been Ito's best student, as he had often boasted in private, and at times in public, or had Jasper's skills faded throughout these years?

In the vacuum of Jasper's mind, Ito had to be both proud and contemptuous of his former charge. That was the only way to think about it.

But a thought like this only ever lasts a moment. Survival is like that: it filters the trivial, the inconsequential and the unnecessary; it gets your thoughts to their points. And the point, in this particular instance, was to find and kill the man who taught him everything he knew.

Jasper funneled his awareness into the channels of his ear canals, proceeding as he was trained to do in such a situation. As he circled the room, the arena of the audio was translated into the realm of the visual: things appeared to him in great detail, the smoke, moving slower and slower, like granules of sand floating in ocean water, he could isolate each and every one of them—each granule, suspended in the air in front of him, measuring the distance between each harmonic layer of sound that Jasper could decipher. And he could decipher them all.

The ability to identify harmonicity—the harmonic relation between sounds—was *on the exam*, per se. He had been tested, examined by Ito himself, and that test continued in this room. Everything he observed inside his mind's eye was sculpted from the fragments of sound collected in his ears and interpreted into the images being projected onto the screen at the front of his imagination.

Footstep: three o'clock, 2.45 feet away, accompanied by a breath, a labored exhale—Ito must be getting older, from the high frequency of the air whistling through his trachea—his head was just under a foot behind the step. He was stepping forward, toward Jasper.

Jasper didn't wait for the next footstep, given away by the sound of his mentor's knee in the air, under the cover of smoke, granules shifting around the joint, the aluminum buttons on his cargo pants' pocket rubbing against the waxed cotton fabric in which they were embedded, scraping ever so slightly. He didn't need to hear the sound of the blade cut through the air; he knew what was coming next—

Jasper jumped out of the line of the strike, the sound of a swinging blade coming after. He leapt over the sword that Ito swung at his legs, looking down upon the blur of the weapon, clearing it with room to spare.

His knee brought him back to the ground as Ito shifted his footing and swung for Jasper's head—

Jasper ducked the blade, reached up and locked Ito's head between his forearm and bicep. He grunted as he threw an unsuspecting Ito over his shoulder, landing Ito hard onto his back. They were close enough to each other now where Jasper's eyes became useful once again. Jasper threw a punch, taking aim at the silhouette of a head, but Ito rolled out of the way. The only thing Jasper caught was the hair on his mentor's chin—and it was a good thing for Ito, because Jasper would've caved in his face.

The momentum of Jasper's punch left his heavy torso hunched over as his face headed toward the floor. Ito whipped his leg, sweeping his student's legs out from under him. Jasper fell, back-flipping into the smoke.

It was Ito's turn to be alone, to simultaneously hunt and be hunted, amidst the haze of the smoke—

He twisted around, shuffling his feet in three-hundred-and-sixty degree patterns; his technique was a lot less surreptitious than Jasper's. It didn't appear as though he was hiding from Jasper. If he could retract the smoke into the shell of its grenade, he might have done so. Either way, he wasn't about to let his guard down.

"You were my most promising student—promise you have yet to fulfill. We need you, Jasper. The program needs you. Come back home."

As Ito continued to circle, wearing the fog as his cloak, its granules settling atop his shoulders like unwanted dandruff, Jasper materialized behind him, wrapping the leftover rope around his former teacher's neck, pulling it tight, choking Ito with the sheer brutality of an animal finishing its prey. Jasper tugged with such strength he lifted Ito's feet off the ground.

Ito attempted to swing the sword in his hand backwards, swiping it blindly and wildly behind his head, sparking it against the wall. Dodging the whirling steel, Jasper blocked the effort with ease, grabbing Ito's wrist and kneeing his hand—knocking the blade from his grip. The weapon clinked to the ground; the blade, a flopping dead silverfish.

Jasper brought Ito's head close to his own, the sides of his lips brushing against the outside of his mentor's ear, "I am home..."

Ito couldn't breath; he didn't try to, because he knew he couldn't. It was clear to both men that his life was slipping from him.

Jasper clutched the rope, pulling it tighter, the strands of the rope biting deeper into the skin of Ito's neck—

Ito inched his hand toward his chest pocket, fumbling with even the easiest of dexterous tasks. He inserted his fingers into the folds of its fabric and attempted to fish something out. The rope fibers squeaked, becoming more and more taut. Jasper's face was aflame with redness, a shade flooded with strength and uninhibited rage, as he depleted the life from his mentor.

The smoke began to dissipate, as though it was timed to abate at this precise second, this moment of reckoning. The image of the two men entangled together became clear to the naked eye.

Ito, approaching the blissful end of consciousness, eventually pulled out what he was attempting to find: a small gadget resembling a flashlight.

He brought the device over his shoulder, gripping onto it weakly, and pointed it at Jasper's face. He jammed his thumb into a button on its side, illuminating the top of the instrument and emitting the sound of an electrical surge—like the sound that accompanies the professional photographer firing off a camera flash—a pattern of light blasted from the device, directly into Jasper's eyes—

Jasper was instantly drawn into the light, drawn into its flicker.

The joints in his arms went slack, loosening his grip on the rope and dropping Ito to the ground. Ito fought desperately to catch his breath. Jasper, his eyes in the midst of glazing over, and the muscles in his back and abdomen melting into nothing, mechanically dropped to his knees. Ito struggled to get back on his feet, finally standing up, leaning over this man, his creation.

Jasper's eyes directed themselves to his sword on the ground. As he reached toward its handle, Ito simply stood there, permitting him to do so. Ito watched Jasper as he picked his weapon up from the floor with one hand, as though in some kind of trance, and used his other to wrap this hand with the rope, tying himself to the handle, securing his grip.

Jasper then turned the tip of the blade toward himself—

He proceeded to shut both his eyes, and as he shut them, Ito did the same. In the midst of his stupor, Jasper managed to whisper:

あなたが現在にカットすると、 将来の漏出.

It was Japanese, the English translating to: "When you cut into the present, the future leaks out." But the words didn't matter. Jasper recited the phrase as though he were reciting a mantra, and like any good mantra, the words meant nothing; what meant something was the light: the *mantra* of the light.

He repeated the utterance three times, but to Jasper, it felt as though he had whispered it both once and a thousand times.

The iteration was the beat—it didn't become the beat, it is, and was, the beat. It would always be the beat. The beat at the beginning, the beat that would end things when the beat stopped—the beat that was meant to stop at this moment. If Jasper were to think one final and absolute thought, the beat would not allow for it; and like the switch of a light being turned off, it was over.

Jasper plunged the blade into his abdomen, carving a deep circle through the expanse of his skin, disemboweling himself as if in an instant. His insides spilled out onto the floor, coating the grime and dusting of dirt that had fallen down from above with the gelatinous glaze of his soul.

The Japanese called it *harakiri*. And that's what he and others were programmed to perform, should the asset be deemed irrecoverable by the agency.

Ito opened his eyes and caught Jasper's body as it fell lifelessly forward. He knelt down on the ground, embracing his fallen student and sheltering his remains from the gore. He wasn't surprised when he noticed Jasper's listless body shaking in his arms. The shaking wasn't a result of Jasper—he was dead, that much was clear. It was Ito's own arms that shook. These were the arms that taught his protégé the black arts that almost brought him to his end.

There was some clarity in the darkness, and that clarity was derived from this one simple truth: the end of anything makes the things around it tremble.

***

In the expanse of the orchard, Paris appeared miniscule as she tore across the field. It was just her and the landscape, until a sniper popped his head out of one of the hatches behind her. He took aim on the moving target and opened fire.

Paris turned, catching sight of the gunman—he may or may not have been shooting to injure, rather than to kill, but it didn't matter; he was still shooting. The detail of this person being one of Cary's people or one of Ito's people was irrelevant, and it became more irrelevant the farther away she got. She hit the ground, tumbling into a roll. The cover of a nearby a tree trunk beckoned her. She obliged its request.

Flecks of bark exploded from behind her head as soon as she shielded herself. She scoped a hatch a few feet in front of her. She sensed some movement from under its cover. As the bullets stopped, she took a long second, and then sprinted toward the hatch as fast as she could.

As she made her approach, another sniper popped his head up, raising the scope of the rifle to his eye—she kicked him swiftly across the face, whipping his head back and to the left, and grabbing his weapon in the process. As the other sniper kept his finger pressed against the trigger, continuing to release his clip of its burden of bullets, Paris hit the ground, aimed, and shot back at her assailant.

Her bullets riddled the top of his chest, blasting his right shoulder from his body, dropping him limply into the hole. She was surprised at the result, a result that in all likelihood equated to the death of another human being. She thought about this, this *result*, but only after she sprung to her feet and continued to run.

Paris navigated the orchard, running from tree to tree. She surveyed the area behind the security of the newfound assault rifle in her hands. In the distance, she glimpsed the coastline that consisted of a small, rickety dock with a handful of fishing boats that looked just as small and rickety.

She breathed a pocket of air into her lungs, dashing toward the port as she exhaled a seismic breath.

***

Ito placed Jasper down on the floor of the bunker with as much respect as he could muster. This was perhaps the most gentle he had ever treated Jasper. To teach one how to survive, one must be taught how to survive—one must practice rigor, vigilance and indifference. As Ito stood over the corpse, he spoke softly into a wrist-mic: "Engage cargo."

The Blackwing Bomber cut through the air above the orchard like an iron phoenix. Inside its cabin, the pilot proceeded to rotate several switches on the dash to three o'clock and then pressed his fingertip to a translucent button, which when depressed began blinking the brightest of reds. The recurrent sound of a wretched buzz accompanied the blinking. The individual steering this monster spoke into the headset built into the side of his helmet, "Cargo engaged… airspace has been cleared… we've gone ghost. Approximately five minutes until the drop."

Ito lowered his wrist to his side. He took his stroboscopic device and tossed it across the room. The diminutive device smashed into several pieces. He bent down, bringing his head close to Jasper's. He brought his fingers to Jasper's closed eyes, running them up over the tops of his eyelids—and he opened them.

The sharp sounds of a helicopter reverberated through the air, each blade cutting into the surf of sound waves and echoing down to the land below. The armored chopper descended upon the area of the orchard that housed the bunker. It lowered a line into the hatch. Just as quick as it was lowered, it was in the midst of being raised, Ito attached to it. The chopper plucked him from the pit of this lifeless void and lifted him into the belly of the aircraft.

At the edge of the dock, Paris cast the lines off a fishing boat—one, and then another—as she watched the chopper retrieve Ito. Once he was safely aboard, the helicopter veered away from the land and headed toward the water. Paris's desperate eyes snapped back to the hatch, and they remained there, waiting for her father to emerge. Then, a rumbling echoed from behind her—

She twisted herself around, looking into the sky, as the Blackwing Bomber emerged from the clouds, inviting itself into the picturesque panorama and approaching the island without discernable discretion.

The bomber steered away from the Pacific Ocean, its starboard wing spearing into the sky above and its port appendage pointing menacingly toward the swathe of land below. "Ten seconds until cargo drop," the pilot muttered into his headset. He flipped another button, the kind that has a switch over the switch, a switch that needs to be flipped up first in order to engage. The level of buzzing increased in both volume and intensity.

The Blackwing Bomber—a metallic cloud of a death machine—retracted the doors in its stomach and released a firestorm of incendiary clusters onto the farmhouse and its surrounding grounds. Paris watched in horror as the entirety of the building, the trees and parched ground erupted into flames.

"No!"

The hits on the building set in motion a series of explosions inside. Fire coursed through the cavernous room of the brain-mapping laboratory, igniting the cylinder of LCD panels, the electrodes, the plethora of high-tech equipment and chemical compounds. The room detonated into sheer oblivion.

The dark shaft of the underground tunnel, at once, became aglow—fire shot through it like a giant roman candle. Everything in its path was incinerated without prejudice.

Jasper remained sprawled on the floor, his limbs listless, but the rest of him somehow triumphant in death as a fireball blew through the door, setting the room and its contents ablaze—

Jasper's body was instantaneously engulfed in flames, the flicker of the fire reflected in his glasslike eyes. There was life in his eyes, but it wasn't his own.

One after the other, the hatches scattered along the grounds erupted into flames like oil geysers tapping the black gold. Paris gazed at the burning hole inside of which she had last seen her father. She was apoplectic, but her instincts—instincts that she inherited from her father—kept her moving. She started the engine on the boat.

She shifted the vessel into gear, increased the throttle and sped out of the dock, cutting the bottom of the boat through the water. She did not look back.

As Paris got a little further out to sea, she seemed to be in the clear. At least from her perspective. However, like her father, she knew better than most: perspective is limited. Without warning, Ito's armored helicopter swooped in front of her, plummeting from the cover of the cotton-candy clouds, and squaring its nose up to her boat—

She was seething, staring into the face of the chopper.

Ito, in its passenger seat, peered down at Paris. Their eyes met once again. It was a standoff—a fairly one-sided one, but a standoff nonetheless—and this time Paris was not about to give an inch.

She pointed her rifle at the chopper and unloaded the weapon into its metallic skin. The aircraft swerved, but her actions were useless; they amounted to more of a protest than an impediment to her oppressors. Paris screamed a savage battle cry as she emptied the ammo from her clip. She continued to engage the trigger of the empty weapon, as though her intent was just as real as the result; bullet, or no bullet, it didn't matter.

Ito looked down at Paris, then turned to the pilot with a tangible level of dispassion: "Fire." The pilot flipped a switch at the top right of the helicopter's control panel and initiated the firing of a missile.

Paris dropped her empty weapon to the floor and listened stoically to the silence in the air. The silence was clear. She began running aft, to the stern of the boat, and leapt over the gunwale as the missile was engaged and fired from above. She was barely in midair as the boat exploded—

Ito surveyed the blast from inside the chopper, its flames obscuring his view as Paris descended into the water. The boat split into endless pieces, scattering a slew of dangerous projectiles into the water around it. From above, the sea below was a contaminated mess: debris, flames, pockets of oil, residual explosions, and presumably a dead body—even though they couldn't see it. Ito was looking for it, silently counting the seconds.

The pilot turned to him, awaiting the next order. Ito nodded, finally, and with finality, "Let's go." The chopper pulled its body up, soaring into the direction from which it came, away from the surface of the water, which left no sign of Paris.

CHAPTER FOURTEEN

O N A TELEVISION, the evening news was in the midst of its primetime broadcast. There was a hint of a reflection on the glass, reflecting the surroundings in which the television was situated. However, it was only a hint. The shapes that could be singled out weren't really shapes; their silhouettes weren't enough to connote any Jungian archetypes or cultural symbols, like the face of Jesus, the swastika, or a .357 Magnum, to name the obvious. These tinges of reflections were mere indications of a living room that revolved around a ubiquitous device. It was a thoroughly anonymous living room, designed via catalog or an online video tutorial. It was a room that in all likelihood looked like a hundred, a thousand, a million other rooms with similar model televisions airing the same, or similar, broadcast.

The surroundings were irrelevant; the focus was the programming. The focus was always on the programming. The female news anchor, an oval-faced blonde in a khaki pantsuit, addressed the viewers at home: "Residents of the Pacific Northwest community of Bainbridge Island have been evacuated." Inside a pop-up window over her epauletted left shoulder, stark images of whitebark pine trees on fire, a coastline covered in grey ash and a legion of National Guardsman barricading roads flashed on the screen. A procession of first responders and fire trucks secured the area.

"Wildfires have ravaged the western side of the island," the anchor continued, "and authorities strongly urge townspeople to seek safety in nearby Seattle. Government ferries will be running three times hourly."

The shot on the screen switched to a close-up of the mustached male anchor—the gender balance to the broadcast—sitting next to his female counterpart.

"Shifting gears to politics," the other anchor enunciated, taking the reins of the news as the devastation remained fresh in the retinas of the viewing audience, "President Rafferty's stunning decision to increase defense spending after months of congressional infighting might be categorized as a three-sixty to most Americans. But as we've learned, this comes as no surprise to many who believe such spending is paramount to national security…and its necessity, a foregone conclusion."

The slick logo for *Allied Precision Electronics* swooped into the window beside the anchor, its introduction to the milieu of the screen obscuring the broadcast's ticker-of-doom streaming across the bottom.

"Grayson Emmett Lowell, the CEO of Allied Precision Electronics, one of our military's chief private contractors, and the manufacturer of the controversial SX-51 Blackwing Bomber, an expense often maligned by President Rafferty in the past, sat down with us for a rare interview."

The program cut to the referenced interview with Grayson Emmett Lowell, the Fortune Five Hundred CEO of A.P.E., who also happened to be *the client* Cary presented his flicker lecture to earlier in an undisclosed conference room. In terms of the camerawork, the corpulent gentleman was shot in a rather claustrophobic medium close-up, mid-shoulders and up, leaving the rest of his body ostensibly to the viewers' imagination.

"I do not fault the opposition over the past several months," Lowell said. "You certainly can't fault those in congress, and until recently, the president, for doing what they're elected to do—that is, standing up for their constituents in this troubling economy. With unemployment the worst we've seen in sixty years—no, I can't blame them, I can't blame them at all." Lowell started to get a bit firmer, his slack jowls tightening, tempering some of that down-home charm. "But you must understand—we all must understand—the global seat of power brings with it not only monumental responsibility, but also an entire globe of enemies. Enemies, to this day, we do not fully understand. To neglect our nation's defense, under any circumstance, is a failure to govern at the most fundamental level."

Lowell leaned forward, bringing his face closer to the camera, "We are a nation at war. It's what, for better or worse, defines us. Pretending we're not is a disservice to the men and women who have died to give this country the freedom we have not only come to expect, but also cherish." He shifted in his seat a little, plastering on a smile, "You see, I'm a product of this country—a product of its coveted American Dream. Born from humble roots, just like so many of you, my granddaddy built himself up from a little bit of nothing, going from planting apple trees to owning, working and running his own orchard."

The broadcast punched into an even tighter shot of Lowell, a visual shift that seemed unnecessary; the previous shot was tight enough.

"And that's why I love this country, and why I feel it's my duty to protect it. I owe it that. I owe my granddaddy that." His smile hardened into something not quite a smile, but not quite a grimace, either—it was something else altogether. "In America, I am the grandson of an apple farmer."

***

SEVERAL MONTHS LATER. Inside the D.I.C. center of operations. Black high heels clacked across the polished floor as a woman pushed a mail cart through the office corridor of the high-rise building. The shoes were reminiscent of the shoes that once frequented Jasper's dreams, his reality, his dream of his reality, but the color was altogether different. It might also be mentioned that the floor was reminiscent of that shiny San Francisco linoleum, but this specific floor was so spotlessly clean that a physician could perform surgical tasks on its surface. The San Francisco floor, in Paris's building near Haight-Ashbury, was far from sterilized and would never, intentionally, serve as a venue for such tasks; however, these echoes remained.

This woman proceeded along her path, distributing envelopes of varying size into the narrow, rectangular boxes on the desks that she passed. She continued nonchalantly down the hall, turning a corner, her face still an object of obscurity.

She brought her cart to a halt in front of the office of Special Agent Hiroshi Ito, his name embedded in the Formica placard on the outside of the door.

Ito sat hunched inside his office, perusing a computer database of names, locations and statuses—perhaps they were his assets. It was clear that the man Ito was, the man Jasper knew him to be, did not belong anywhere near the confines of an office building. There was likely some truth to the notion that part of Ito, a rather essential part, was left behind in that bunker alongside Jasper's remains.

In a manner of speaking, the room smelled of death—the death of a man whose job it was to outsmart it.

There was a knock at the door. Ito looked up from his computer, removing the black acetate glasses perched on the tip of his nose. "Yes. Please come in."

The door opened. The woman grabbed a thick envelope from the cart and walked inside. As Ito looked up, the woman approached—

"This was messengered over."

The woman was Paris Robertson, disguised in rather nondescript mailroom attire, adorned with the requisite credentials looped to a lanyard around her neck. Before Ito could begin to react, Paris pulled her *tessen*—her iron spiked fan—from the envelope and extended its silk folds.

Ito's eyes widened as she swiftly whipped the weapon toward him, driving its hidden spikes into his throat. She held it for a moment, peering into his eyes and squeezing his Adam's apple between the blades, as he asphyxiated on the bodily fluids leaking from the arteries inside his neck.

She removed the spikes, fast.

Ito collapsed in his chair, almost as fast as she extracted the weapon from his body. Blood cascaded down the front of him like a waterfall adorning the garden of some corporate headquarters—it was as constant and as matter-of-fact.

Paris stood over Ito, her father's daughter. The opening riff to Sonic Youth's *100%* began to reverberate inside her brain as if her neurons tripped the song into playback—it was as though it were the theme of the moment, the background music, the non-diegetic score. Didn't a moment like this, she thought to herself, deserve such audio accompaniment? Didn't it deserve a soundtrack?

The dissonant feedback continued to linger as she retreated into the office bathroom down the hall, rigging the door shut with the heel of her shoe and throwing her lanyard along with its phony identification into the trash receptacle adjacent to the stainless steel sink. The sound of the song slowly began to sync itself into harmony with the other notes, notes that didn't want to get along with each other, notes that would never get along, unless they were forced to.

"Can you forgive the boy who… shot you in the head? Or should you get a gun and… go and get revenge?"

Paris looked at herself in the mirror. She let her hair down from its bun and tossed her black locks behind the cusps of her shoulders. She surveyed the contours of her face—the bridge of her nose, the curves of her cheeks, the slope of her forehead—looking for her father. As much as she could feel, she thought, the spirit of her dad, of Jasper, of Sam, or something akin to a genetic footprint within her DNA, the man was as much a stranger inside her now as he was when he was in her life.

But it didn't matter. She was her father's daughter; there was legacy to consider, there were wrongs that needed to be made right.

She took the tessen from her pocket, extended its blood-soaked folds, and laid the outstretched fan atop the sink. Under a certain light, such a gesture might be seen as a sacrifice, an offering to the God who created her father, and who, in ways too numerous to count, created her.

She grabbed her shoe from beneath the door, placed it back on her foot and hastened out of the bathroom.

"One hundred percent of my love… up to you true star."

Outside the entrance to the agency's headquarters, Paris exited through the revolving doors of the modern skyscraper and sauntered down the sidewalk. She sauntered because that was how someone walked to this specific soundtrack when it echoed within the amphitheater of one's own head: the soundtrack of angst, of discordance, of birthright, of the beat, and ultimately of revenge. It was the soundtrack of youth's revenge against the old, against the establishment and all of its trappings. It was the soundtrack of youth's revenge against everything that came before.

"But I've been around the world a million times, and all you men are slime. It's the gun to my head, goodbye I am dead, Wastewood rockers is time for cryin', hey!"

She blended into the stream of pedestrians on the sidewalk and extended her arm in the air to hail a cab. She hopped into the backseat of the first taxi that pulled to the curb.

She closed the door and the car drove away, undetected, into the intestines of the anonymous city.

ABOUT THE AUTHOR

WILLIAM DICKERSON graduated from The College of The Holy Cross with a Bachelor's Degree in English and received his Master of Fine Arts in Directing from The American Film Institute. His feature film *Detour*, which he wrote and directed, was hailed as an "Underground Hit" by *The Village Voice*, an "emotional and psychological roller-coaster ride" by *The Examiner*, and nothing short of "authentic" by *The New York Times*.

His award-winning work has been recognized by film festivals across the country.

His first novel, *No Alternative*, was declared, "a sympathetic coming-of-age story deeply embedded in '90s music" by Kirkus Reviews. He recently adapted the book into a motion picture starring Michaela Cavazos, Conor Proft, Chloe Levine, Kathryn Erbe and Harry Hamlin. Its soundtrack features songs from Grunge-era standouts such as Mudhoney, Failure, sElf, Superdrag, Lisa Loeb, Sebadoh and others.

He lives in Los Angeles, California.

For more information about William's books, films and upcoming projects, check out his website:
www.williamdickersonfilmmaker.com

9 780985 188658